Dear Mit:

. . . Glad to hear the braces are finally off. I couldn't do anything about my freckles—you'll soon see for yourself . . . Why didn't we ever go out together in college? After all, you were the first girl I ever kissed—something you know full well because I bungled the job badly . . . see you soon, Mit. I hope you've given up that horrible perfume you wore in high school. Mrs. Creighton used to open the window in science class to keep us from being asphyxiated! What was it called, Midnight with the Camels?

Colly

Dear Rotten Rankin,

You're wrong, Colly, Mrs. Creighton never opened the window to get rid of my delicious, wonderful Midnight in Cairo perfume. Just for that, I'll wear some to lunch! . . . As for the kissing, I never knew you bungled the job. How was I to make a comparison? At the time I thought it was the most wonderful kiss in the world. I dreamed of becoming Mrs. Colly Rankin and moving to the South Seas to watch you pearl-dive. Funny how life never turns out the way you expect it. . . .

Mit

WHAT ARE *LOVESWEPT* ROMANCES?

They are stories of true romance and touching emotion. We believe those two very important ingredients are constants in our highly sensual and very believable stories in the *LOVESWEPT* line. Our goal is to give you, the reader, stories of consistently high quality that may sometimes make you laugh, sometimes make you cry, but are always fresh and creative and contain many delightful surprises within their pages.

Most romance fans read an enormous number of books. Those they truly love, they keep. Others may be traded with friends and soon forgotten. We hope that each *LOVESWEPT* romance will be a treasure—a "keeper." We will always try to publish

LOVE STORIES YOU'LL NEVER FORGET
BY AUTHORS YOU'LL ALWAYS REMEMBER

The Editors

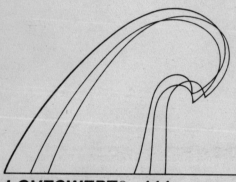

LOVESWEPT® • 111

Sara Orwig
Dear Mit

BANTAM BOOKS
TORONTO • NEW YORK • LONDON • SYDNEY • AUCKLAND

DEAR MIT

A Bantam Book / October 1985

LOVESWEPT® and the wave device are registered trademarks of Bantam Books, Inc. Registered in U.S. Patent and Trademark Office and elsewhere.

ISBN 0-553-21726-7

Published simultaneously in the United States and Canada

Bantam Books are published by Bantam Books, Inc. Its trademark, consisting of the words "Bantam Books" and the portrayal of a rooster, is Registered in U.S. Patent and Trademark Office and in other countries. Marca Registrada. Bantam Books, Inc., 666 Fifth Avenue, New York, New York 10103.

PRINTED IN THE UNITED STATES OF AMERICA

O   0 9 8 7 6 5 4 3 2 1

To Carolyn, who gave all her petunias room
to grow. Thank you, thank you . . .

One

December 11

Marilyn:

Happy holidays from the north side of town. Saw your pic in the paper for Friends of the Zoo. It didn't identify you by name, but I'd know those big eyes anywhere. The goofy zoo hat hid your hair! Know all the animals love you. Podge loved you more than he did me, but then a nine-year-old boy may not have been a cat's best friend. I guess you've seen Dad's picture in the paper and read about the bank foreclosure. It's a mess, but that's not why I'm writing. It's been some ten years since we got together and compared notes. Are you married? A mother? I'm not either one. Know you're laughing as much now as you always did at my jokes.

Want to meet for lunch and go over old times? I'll call after the first of the year, once the dust settles from the holidays. If I get your hubby, I'll just explain I'm the skinny, freckled kid who used to live next door and would lob mudballs at you to hear you scream. (I never really tried to hit you.)

Merry New Year, babe!

A voice from the past,

Colly

December 21

Dear Colly:

How nice to hear from you, and lunch would be fun. It's been much too long. What happened to the quiet moments when we'd stand around beneath the pear tree and try to think of what we could do next? Life's so hectic. I'm not a mother, and I'm not married, just so damned busy trying to hold things together. Let's make a pact like we used to—lunch together, and we won't discuss any problems—okay?

I'm sorry about your dad's difficulties. Surely it will work out all right.

Merry Christmas, Colly. Our folks shouldn't have moved so far apart. And that year we were both in college together seems a long time ago now.

Love,

Mit

March 4

Dear Mit:

Hell's bells, it's March, and we still haven't had lunch! I've tried to call you forty-one times but couldn't catch you at home. You do live on Newblock Avenue, don't you? So, busy lady, how about lunch, Friday, March 23, noon? At the

Plaza? Now, you can reach me—not only do I have a phone that occasionally I'm home to answer, but I also have an answering machine at the office. Take a second from your busy schedule, dial this number, and say yes or no. I'll know who and why. Can't wait. Do you still wear braces?

Colly
555–6454

March 16

Dear Freckles:

You're still lobbing mudballs to hear me scream—don't ask about braces! I'm sure I was the only female enrolled in the university who wore braces, and you know how I hated them! I called, and your phone wasn't working. I called, and your line was busy. I called, and your answering machine wasn't picking up. I'm sorry, but March 23 is out because I have to pick up oysters at the airport. How about a week later, March 30? Same time and same place?

Screams and gnashing teeth . . . and if you want to go out with me, don't mention braces!

Mit

March 24

Dear Mit:

I wouldn't lob a mudball at you now! Braces you can get rid of, freckles you can't, so who's throwing mudballs and hitting the target? I'd hide my freckles under a beard, but I don't have time to grow one before we get together. (Or do I?)

You're meeting oysters at the airport? I always knew there was something strange about you and your family. Are the oysters staying with you long or is this a short visit?

When the oysters shove off, or whatever they do, how about the following week, April 6? The Plaza is closed for remodeling. Let's try Pirate's Cove. The fried chicken is scrumptious, and, as I recall, you can put away a whole half without batting an eye.

Hot rolls and honey too. Say hello to the oysters for me. I'll try to bleach my freckles. Do you still have short curls?

Colly

March 29

Dear Mr. Rankin:

I would like to stomp my feet and yell—or fall in the chair and laugh. Why am I thinking about going out with you when you are snide, infuriating, and idiotic! People who live with glass brains shouldn't toss unkind remarks. My curls grew out. Now my hair is almost as long as yours was in college. Have you finally cut it, or is it dragging the street?

I can put away half a chicken, you say! Do you remember any of the nice things about me? Like how I'd save the wings for you and bring them over after dinner? I guess I hoped they would help fatten up your knobby knees. Instead, it all went to your size twelve feet. I presume you've grown into your feet by now.

What happened to the doll you were going to marry? Are you still engaged, and is she joining us? She seemed very sweet—far too sweet for the likes of you.

I had to pick up boxes of oysters at the airport because I work at a restaurant that is also in the catering business. I run fun errands like that. What do you do? As I remember, you wanted to grow up to be a pearl diver. Since we live in the middle of the U.S. in landlocked Oklahoma, I suppose you gave up pearl diving for another career. I can't recall what you majored in at college except football. I thought you'd turn pro after graduation.

Sorry, April 6 is out. I have to ride in a hot-air balloon the morning of April 6, and it might not come down in time for lunch. The next day? April 7 at twelve o'clock at Pirate's Cove.

Will we recognize each other?
Mit

April 2

Dear Mit:
It's a good thing you're out of reach. Knobby knees, long hair, big feet. I'm not going to tell you which of those I still have. You'll have to see for yourself.

Maybe. I don't know if we'll ever get to lunch with your busy schedule.

You're catering something in a hot-air balloon? Or are you dropping packets of food? If I step out onto the patio, can I see you go by? I think your life has changed since we stood under the pear tree.

Sorry, I can't make it April 7. I have a meeting. How about April 18? I have an office—no pearl diving. I'm in demolition. Sometimes I don't work in an office, though. Sometimes I tear down offices.

And I did play pro ball. All that time I'd think, "Mit is cheering me on like she used to do on the block at home." Hah! You didn't know I was alive. Another disillusionment.

My hair isn't dragging the street. I can't picture you with long hair. Why didn't we ever go out together in college? After all, you're the first girl I ever kissed, which you know full well since I bungled the job badly.

Happy ballooning. Are you taking the oysters with you? I guess you finally outgrew your silly fear of heights. I think your life is more interesting than mine. Friends of the Zoo, balloons, oysters . . . who's the guy in your life? He must love your long eyelashes.

Do we have a date?

Colly

April 12

Dear Mr. Colin Corinthian Rankin:

I still don't understand your name, but I finally learned to spell it. No, we don't have a date. Sorry. I have a luncheon to cater that day. Shall we try for after Easter? I'm so busy around a holiday.

There's no important guy in my life. I'm sure your life is interesting. Demolition? You destroy things?

I didn't know you bungled the job. How was I to make a comparison? At the time I thought it was the most wonderful kiss in the world. I dreamed of becoming Mrs. Colly Corinthian Rankin and moving to the South Seas to watch you pearl-dive. Life never turns out the way we expect it to.

I'm glad you like my eyelashes. I was riding in the hot-air balloon because it says EAT AT HICKS across the balloon, and they're filming a commercial for the restaurant. I'm still terrified of heights, but it was either go up in the balloon or lose a tidy bonus in pay. I didn't throw food from the balloon because I was too busy clinging tightly to the sides.

Oops, sorry. I didn't mean to spill my drink on the letter, but I'm in bed, it's half past two, and if I don't write now, I won't get it done. Sorry.

Night,

M.

April 30

Dear M.W.:

Wine in bed at half past two? You *have* changed! If there's no guy, how do you keep so damned busy?

Corinthian was one of Mother's little pet words, and it is a deep, dark secret. I can just imagine the guys I work with if they got hold of that, so keep it *quiet*.

Please don't be an ecology freak. They haunt my life. I earn a legitimate wage tearing down structures I'm hired to tear down. Your letter had a nasty tone. You'll be sorry if I'm blown to bits someday. You'll wish you'd been nicer. You'll miss me.

Remember how we used to stand at the fence and yell that sort of stuff at each other? Until you'd run off crying and your mother would call my mother and I'd catch the devil over it! Snitch.

You work for Hicks Bar and Grill? Which one? They have the best mesquite-grilled steaks and swordfish in town. Too bad I couldn't ride in the balloon with you and hold your hand like I used to do when we'd climb up on the garage roof.

What do you do with your time? You're doing something to keep you away from the phone. In all honesty, I haven't been around much these last two weeks. Work's piling up, and right now I'm procrastinating doing my bookkeeping by writing to you. Maybe we'll just be pen pals. Except I want to see you. I have to see those long eyelashes again. And big green eyes. How come someone hasn't succumbed to those big green eyes by now? Are you holding out on me?

The sweet little gal I was engaged to didn't want to have to worry about a pro football player, she didn't want to leave Oklahoma, she didn't want to do this or that, and I didn't want to settle down at Daddy's firm, so we parted company. She's married now, has two kids. Occasionally we pass in the street and it finally means nothing. There, I've caught you up on my secrets. Your turn. You're being very evasive about your personal life. For someone who used to hold me down and tell me everything Patsy Tyler had said to you at school, you've gotten mighty quiet.

We're heading into May, the jonquils are blooming, and I'm beginning to date my secretary. Nothing serious, and I've told her about you. I should have her type these letters, but I don't think she would appreciate or understand our relationship. She's nice. And attractive. Leah's her name. Who's the guy in your life? There's got to be one. No one with the legs you had in college, those gorgeous eyelashes, and your incredible green eyes could be without a man hovering somewhere nearby.

Shall we try for:

1) May 21 at Thomasina's Palace?
2) May 22 or 23 at Aunt Sugar's Cafeteria?
3) May 24 at The Corner?
4) May 25 at Matt's Old Shoppe?

Drop a line or call. Call my office number, and you can tell Leah or my answering machine.

See you soon. I hope you've given up that horrible perfume you wore in high school. Mrs. Creighton used to have to open the window after your science class, and I don't think you ever knew it was because of that stuff you wore.

Does anyone else call you Mit?

Colly

May 6

Dear Rotten Rankin:

It wasn't wine in bed—it was grape juice! How do I keep busy? I thought we agreed to leave out the problems, so I can't answer that.

I'll come stand on the corner where you're working and yell Colly Corinthian Rankin if you keep saying some of those things you've been saying to me! I'm not an ecology freak, but demolition sounds so destructive. And dangerous. I guess it comes naturally, though—I remember you set fire to your doghouse when you were seven. So I was a snitch! Well, Rotten Rankin, you were a bully. Picking on a little girl who was four years younger and half your size and weight. You deserved more than you got! There were plenty of times I didn't snitch, if you'll crank up your old brain and remember. Like when you broke Mr. Heely's window, or when you let the air out of Mrs. Knudson's tires, or when you let the Rileys' chow in the yard with the Marshalls' pedigreed Doberman (the results of which you always called the Chobermans!). I kept a complete and loyal silence even when grilled intensely at home! So don't call me a snitch! The things I could tell on you! There are people in this town who would still like to know who the culprit was . . . so watch your step!

I work at the original Hicks Bar and Grill on Tenth Street. Let's not eat there, even if they do have the best food in town. I need to get away.

Someone did succumb. I didn't mean to mislead you when I said I wasn't married—I'm widowed. It's Marilyn Whitaker Pearson. No children.

I date occasionally, but it's no big deal. And Mrs. Creighton did *not* open the window to get rid of the smell of my wonderful, delicious Midnight in Cairo perfume! Just for that, I'll wear some to lunch.

And—now comes the *Big Surprise* —I think we're finally going to get together. I can make it May 22 to Aunt Sugar's Cafeteria (ugh—I don't like cafeterias—even after all these years they still remind me of Poe Elementary) or, better yet, I can meet you May 24 at The Corner. I love hamburgers (as you may recall).

How do you remember all those things about me? I suppose the same way I remember so many things about you. I guess our childhood was special. I don't know where I put the car keys ten minutes ago, but I can recall with perfect clarity idiotic things from long ago—like the time you talked me into walking over to Simpson's Pond and going skinny-dipping. It's a wonder we weren't bitten by a copperhead. Two little kids in that mudhole . . . my mother would have fainted dead away if she'd known. But I'm digressing. You know, Colly, it's been fun to write. I've never written letters much. It was such a good time when we were growing up. I hope we don't disillusion each other. I want to see your long brown hair, your freckles, your big feet (I can skip your knobby knees), and your nice blue eyes. Why didn't we stay together, grow up, get married, and live happily ever after?

I guess because it would have been too logical. Ask Leah to join us if you like. She might as well learn about your dark past now.

Back to my perfume. How can you talk? You, who cut off the dead skunk's tail and carried it stuffed in your hip pocket until it almost gassed the entire third grade? And that time in fourth grade when you used to rub bacon rind on your hair to try and straighten out the waves. Ugh. That's why I tried to outrun you every morning on the way to school.

I can't wait to see you. Will we recognize each other or should we wear carnations in our lapels? Or are you still slinking around in T-shirts and sandals? You must have had to give up your sandals to work in demolition.

I'm going to miss our letters. No, no one else calls me Mit. Does anyone else call you Rotten Rankin?

Love,
M.W.P.

May 11

Dear Muzzy Mit:

No one calls me Rotten Rankin—so watch out. (It's better than Colly Corinthian). I'm sorry you're widowed. That's rough.

I got your call on my answering machine. My, you've developed a nice voice. It's just right—that squeaky nasal twang, which made you sound like a mouse with a cold, is gone.

Whoopee! Lunch at The Corner on May 24. I'm all aflutter! I still have your old Captain Flakey Oats Glow-in-the-Dark Magic Ring. Want me to bring it and return it to you?

You may not have to miss our letters. I'm through here the first of June and moving on to a new job, so you can still write to me. And vice versa. I don't think we'll need carnations in our lapels. (You wear lapels?) You have long legs, big green eyes, black hair, and dark eyelashes that are so-o-o long. Right?

My hair isn't long. And I don't use bacon rind on it. I gave up and let it wave. The freckles and big feet and blue eyes you should recognize. And to clinch the matter, due to my job, I now have a nasty scar across my temple. I'm a little battered with time. (There's a touch of revolting gray in the waves too. Kid of twenty-nine, can you believe I'm thirty-three?)

One tooth is missing, but you can't tell that unless you're up close and I laugh. That's from a car wreck, and one of these days I'll get a false tooth, but I haven't taken the time and can't before May 24. I won't wear a T-shirt and sandals. Just for you.

If you wear your Midnight with the Camels perfume, I'll know you instantly, but they'll have to close the restaurant. Try another perfume, please. I have a strong stomach, but not that strong.

I thought the fuss they raised about the skunk's tail was entirely unreasonable. That was a neat tail.

Oh, Mit, what fun it was! And it's fun to look back just a few times on those days.

Leah declined. She said she isn't interested in my life before I reached voting age. Can't imagine why.

I'm not so generous. Don't ask that "occasional" guy. I want you to myself.

I'd forgotten the Chobermans. Remember, the Tandys took one—meanest dog that ever trod the earth. How that mutt hated me. He should've been nicer, without me he wouldn't have entered the world. I wonder if the other pups were that ornery.

If you'll go skinny-dipping with me again, I'll find a clear pond. One without copperheads. Promise.

We should have gotten married and lived happily ever after, but I thought I was so old at twenty-two, I couldn't wait for a youngster of eighteen to grow up. Besides, as I recall that freshman year in college, you were IN LOVE with some creep who had an extremely handsome face and a body to match. And a big empty space where his brain should have been. By the time you broke up with him and came to cry on my shoulder, Jen was in my life and I couldn't see anyone else, especially not a kid who was only a freshman. (I had a little space between the ears then too.)

Oh boy, oh boy, see you May 24! Don't stand me up, Mit. I'll roll on the floor and cry.

Colly

Marilyn Whitaker lowered the familiar letter and gazed across the lobby of the restaurant, looking at the rustic decor, knotty-pine paneling, antique posters and pictures. Old musical instruments hung on the walls; a dented French horn and a tarnished saxophone flanked a window while high ceiling fans stirred the cool air.

Her stomach fluttered with excitement and she looked down again at Colin's bold scrawl, then glanced at her watch. She had arrived early; Colly was late.

She felt a lump in her throat for old times, for the years between, for Colly's fun letters that would end now. She smoothed her slim-fitting light blue cotton skirt and short-sleeved red blouse with the collar turned up. Shaking her shoulder-length black hair away from her face, she stared through the wide archway at the darkened restaurant, where small lamps glowed on the tables and tiny vases of jonquils and red tulips brightened the room.

"Marilyn."

The word was a touch, a hot, syrupy brush that stroked across her senses and fanned them with heat. Her heart slammed against her ribs and bounced back while her temperature rose by degrees. His voice was husky, so husky. She had forgotten. A hand settled on her shoulder as she stood up and turned to look into deep blue eyes.

He was so damned handsome! Shock struck her. She had been expecting a kid, not the man standing before her. A man with broad, powerful shoulders that were emphasized by his white shirt. A man who had a firm jaw, thick wavy brown hair, slim hips covered with dark blue slacks. A man who was looking at her in a way that made her pulse stop. Never before had Colin Rankin looked at her the way he was now.

Slowly, his gaze drifted down. And he'd said she had long eyelashes! she thought with amazement. His were thick and long and shadowed his cheekbones as they lowered. Beneath his gaze she trembled while every nerve quivered in response.

"Holy Detroit! Muzzy Mit, you've grown up!" The words were innocuous, the tone wasn't. The tone was pure caress; in his blue eyes was a blatant masculine approval. And then she was in his arms.

His arms were strong and sure around her. He smelled like the fresh scent of the old Rankin pear tree when it bloomed in the spring. She squeezed her eyes closed and held him as if for those few seconds she could hold her memories, hold a time when life was a joy with no complications, no sad yesterdays or terrifying tomorrows.

"Lord, you smell nice," he murmured in her ear.

She couldn't trust her voice to speak. Then she opened her eyes, saw someone across the lobby staring at her, and common sense returned. She pulled away with a shaky laugh.

"We're causing a scene."

"Who cares?" He held her at arm's length and studied her again, his blue eyes alight with pleasure.

"May I show you to a table?" A hostess in red gingham stood a few feet away, smiling at Colly and waiting.

"For two," he answered easily while his eyes never left Marilyn.

"This way, please."

Marilyn followed the hostess and Colly fell into step behind her. She was intensely aware of him walking so close behind, and her back tingled from her nape straight down her spine. She shook her head, letting the soft pageboy of black hair swirl across her shoulders. They reached a corner booth, and she slid into a seat, watching as Colly sat down opposite her. In defiance of reason, she wanted to reach over and touch him. He was the most marvelous sight on earth, she thought.

"Would you care for a drink?" the waitress asked.

"Two colas," he answered with an inquiring look at Marilyn.

"That's fine," she said, barely aware of the question as she took in his deeply tanned skin, the golden highlights in his hair.

After the waitress left, he asked, "Still a teetotaler?"

"Still. But you can have a drink."

He shook his head. "Not good for my stomach."

There was a moment of silence as they looked at

each other. He said softly, "Lord-a-mercy, Miss Percy, you turned into one good-looking woman."

"Thank you, Colin Corinthian," she answered, glowing with happiness.

"Oh, please!"

She laughed. "You too. My goodness, you're handsome, Colly."

"This face?" He wrinkled his nose.

"You're—" She bit off the words. Sexy, she decided. An extremely appealing man.

"Yes?"

She blushed. "Very handsome."

"My, oh, my! Why do I get the feeling that isn't what you started to say?"

She wriggled, remembering suddenly how they'd always known each other so well they could guess the other's thoughts. "I'm just making comparisons. Your freckles are gone."

"Not really, look close." He leaned over the table and she felt suddenly breathless. What was the matter with her? He was only Colly. Rotten Rankin. Her breathing shouldn't alter over pesky Rotten Rankin. But his eyes were so intense, so blue, and fringed thickly by dark lashes. He didn't look like skinny ol' Rotten Rankin anymore.

"And I've got freckles on my shoulders," he added in his deep, lazy drawl that stroked her nerves like a hot summer wind. "Want to see?"

His question startled her, and she looked up to see the crinkles fanning from the corners of his eyes.

She laughed as he sat back. "You haven't changed—you're still Rotten Rankin."

"I'd forgotten all those things you wrote to me about. We had a good time, didn't we?"

The waitress placed two glasses in front of them along with the menus.

"What would you like, Mit?"

To listen to your voice all the time, she thought, then blinked in surprise. She turned her attention to the menu, but it took another full minute before she could focus on the printed words and forget Colly.

"I'll have a mushroom burger."

"Want nachos, shrimp, a salad?"

She shook her head. "No thanks, a burger is plenty."

He took the menu from her hands and placed it with his on top of the table. "Midnight with the Camels. You're not wearing that today."

"Midnight in Cairo. Thank goodness you're not wearing bacon rind." She looked at his soft brown hair that fell across his forehead in waves. A few gray hairs were discernible. The scar was a thin line across his temple, white against his tanned skin. "What building are you going to demolish here?"

"I've already done the job. You didn't read about it or see it on the ten o'clock news? It was the old Canton Building."

"Oh, no! Colly, it had all that decorative work—"

"I was just doing the job I was paid to do. If I'd turned it down, someone else would have been hired, Mit. I'm not the owner or the city who decided it should go."

She smiled. "Sorry. That's dangerous work. Suppose something falls on you?"

"It keeps the boredom out of my life."

"How on earth did you get into demolition?"

"I played pro ball for two years, then injured my knee and couldn't play. A chance came up to work for a demolition company, with the opportunity to buy the business if I liked it. I took it." He held out his hands. "So here I am. How did you get into the restaurant business?"

"It's a job. So here I am."

"You're being damned evasive."

The waitress appeared, and Colly gave their orders. "One mushroom burger, fries, one cheeseburger and fries. Two coffees with cream."

Marilyn enjoyed watching him, listening to his resonant voice that was sexy just ordering sandwiches. The waitress smiled at Colly, took the menus, and left.

"How on earth did you remember I drink cream in my coffee? I'd just started drinking it that freshman year in college."

"I haven't forgotten the slightest thing about you."

"Oh, no!"

He laughed and fished in his pocket. "Hold out your hand, darling."

Every nerve in her body responded to his request. She knew he was teasing, that he meant nothing personal, but his voice, those special words had the most remarkable effect on her. She held out her hand. She suspected she would have done anything that his husky, sensual voice had asked.

He touched the glittering diamond on her finger, the plain gold band. "The other hand, Mit."

He took her right hand in his, and she looked down at his large, tanned fingers. He turned her hand over, palm down, held her ring finger, and slipped on a ring.

Her pulse drummed like hailstones on a tin roof.

She closed her eyes for one fleeting moment and felt the ring sliding over her finger. If only—

Marilyn shook her head and opened her eyes. What was wrong with her? Every time she heard Colly's sexy voice her brain seemed to shut off. She looked down at the dark green stone in the center of a white plastic ring.

"My Captain Flakey ring! You've had it all these years!"

In a prayerful pose, he held his hands palms together beneath his firm jaw. "Forgive me. I just couldn't resist keeping it, Mit. I wore it until I outgrew it."

She laughed and looked at it on her finger. "Remember how I'd put it in the sun to let it absorb light all afternoon, then go out after dark to scare Sinbad with it?"

"Your dumb cat was too lazy to get worked up over a glowing green stone."

"Don't you call my cat dumb."

"He was, and mine was too smart to fall for that trick. So, will you be on television soon?"

"I'm not on television," she responded, confused by the quick change of subject.

"The hot-air balloon commercial?"

"Oh, I forgot. It should start running in July."

"Shucks. I'll be living in Dallas then."

"Tearing down something there?"

"Yes. An old apartment building."

"You have an aunt there, don't you?"

He groaned. "Don't mention Aunt Phoebe, please. That woman would try the patience of a saint, which I'm not. Mit, let's go skinny-dipping tonight. I wasted my time looking for turtles when we went before."

She laughed, but a faint blush colored her cheeks as she had a brief vision of swimming nude with the gorgeous man seated across from her. "Now I know better than to go skinny-dipping with you," she said.

"It might be more fun than last time," he said, leaning back in the booth. His knee brushed against hers lightly.

She shifted away a fraction, noticing his smile as she did. His voice was playing arpeggios on her nerves, she thought, and each contact with his eyes was like a brush against a live wire. Invisible sparks danced on her spine.

"Let's go back to Acorn Avenue and look at the old houses, Mit. I suppose you've seen them often, since you live here."

Before she could answer, he said quickly, "You haven't gone back."

"You can never go back," she said softly. "No, I haven't seen them. It seems like so long ago."

"Let's go today. One look at the past. Maybe like the Ghost of Christmas Past, it will change our future."

"You're tempting fate, Colly."

"One look for old times' sake."

"If it takes us six months to get together again—"

"I mean now, today. Do you have to go back to work this afternoon?"

"No, I have the afternoon off," she answered, wondering what he would think if he knew it was the first afternoon she had taken off in over two months. And that she had taken the evening off from her second job at Jose's Chili House.

"I can take off the rest of the day too." He leaned forward again. "How about it? After lunch we go back to Acorn."

"All right, but—"

"Shh." He touched her lips with his finger, and her skin all but sizzled with smoke rising from it. "No buts. Today is yesterday, memories. All the good ones. The Chobermans, the pear tree, Poe Elementary, Elmwood High, Midnight in Cairo—all the funny things. We won't remember pimples and braces and skinned knees and fights, just the good things. Let's step through the Looking Glass back into time for a few hours. Tomorrow, Cinderella, the ball will be over. I'll move to Dallas on the first of June, you'll go out with the occasional man, and our lives will part. So let's snatch a few hours together in midstream."

How could she refuse? Marilyn wondered. But would it be another pull on her heart, another big ache to look back on things best forgotten because they could never be again?

"Sure, Colin Corinthian," she said in a sultry, teasing voice. "How can I resist your offer?"

Instead of the reaction she expected—another of his flip comebacks—he sobered and drew a deep breath, looking at her intently with an unmistakable curiosity in his eyes.

"I was teasing," she whispered.

"Yeah, babe," he said in a husky drawl that made her even more aware of his masculinity.

The waitress appeared with platters of fat hamburgers and golden fries. She placed bottles of mustard and ketchup on the table and spoke to Colly. "Anything else, sir?"

He cocked an eye at Marilyn, she shook her head, and he smiled at the waitress. "That's all, thanks."

Marilyn watched him smile. It was marvelous. The

waitress all but purred, and Marilyn could understand her reaction. When the waitress had gone, Marilyn said, "You have a remarkable effect on women."

"Thank goodness you said women." He let out a long breath and pinned her beneath another searching stare. "I have a remarkable effect, huh?"

Why had she said that to him? she thought. Her mind searched frantically for some way to turn the conversation around. "I don't see a missing tooth."

He stared at her a moment longer, then said, "I'm glad. I'm not going to show it to you either. You'll have to take this smile as is."

"You have a dazzling 'as is' smile. How come when we were kids I noticed your freckles, knobby knees, and big feet, and missed your smile?"

"Your priorities are different now. How come I noticed your curls and long lashes and missed . . ." His words trailed off as his gaze lowered to her breasts, and she felt her body's response instantly.

"Colly!"

He grinned, and she snapped, "You're making me crazy!"

"That's a surprise?"

"Hardly. You should've brought Leah along and let her see the real you."

"This is a hell of a lot more fun." Then a funny look crossed his face and she arched her eyebrows.

"What's wrong?" she asked.

"Nothing."

"Colly, you're holding out on me. Shame, shame."

He laughed. "We can still do it, can't we? Read each other's minds?"

"Yes, I suppose so, to a degree. I don't know what you're holding out, just that you are."

"Well, I was surprised that it's a lot more fun to be with you than it is to be with Leah. I'd thought she was fun."

"Well, for Pete's sake, I'm not going to ruin your dating Leah," she said with far more calmness than she felt. A sudden panic gripped her. *We can't have lots of fun, Colly. Please, no. I can't cope with that.* "This is just a few hours, one afternoon," she said firmly, trying to ignore her skipping pulse.

"Yeah, sure. Want mustard?"

"Please."

"Can we talk about each other and the present?" he asked lightly as he handed her the mustard and their fingers brushed.

"If you'd like, but it might be more fun not to. Tell me about your present. You've torn down the Canton Building and you're ready to move on. Are you a nomad or do you have a permanent address?"

"A nomad, really. Maybe that's why it's been so nice to write to you, and try and find my roots. After the twenty-third move, I stopped counting."

Her hand held the bottle in midair. "Oh, Colly, that's terrible!"

"Why?"

"You should be married and settled and have kids and have a house like the one you grew up in."

"You don't."

She blushed. "Touché." She spread mustard on the bun. "Are you happy moving around?"

"I don't know. I was for a time." He looked away and she realized that she hurt for him. The thought of him wandering from town to town disturbed her.

Then she told herself she was being ridiculous. He was handsome, self-employed, doing what he wanted. Yet his voice had a sober tone.

"I went a little wild after losing Jen." Blue eyes settled on her and she saw a painful look in their depths. "I lived high and wild while I played ball. Fast cars, fast women, the whole bit . . . The first year after pro ball I was even in a movie."

"No kidding?"

His white teeth flashed. "I love the way you take these things. The producer saw something in me besides knobby knees."

"You can act? Well, I guess you can at that. Goodness knows, you had some practice trying to talk your way out of the scrapes you got yourself into."

"I think they wanted beefcake more than talent. My big shoulders and not my brain."

"Then you must have been perfect. What was the movie?"

His grin widened. "How could you have missed it: *Agar from Antares*."

She giggled and tried to hide it behind her hamburger.

"Mit!" he said in a threatening voice.

"Who were you?" she asked, looking down at her plate and trying to smother her laughter.

"I was the star, Agar."

She choked and coughed and held her napkin in front of her face. He snatched it away and in mock sternness said, "I'll get even. Just wait!"

She laughed. "Is it on late-night television?"

"Lordy, I hope not!"

"I'll watch for it."

They ate in silence a moment. "I'm sorry about your folks, Mit."

"Thanks. Thanks for the flowers too."

"I got your note each time. It seems impossible they're no longer living."

"I know."

"You know, I bid on this job so I could come stay in town while my dad fights this bank scandal. It's really a mess. I can't believe my dad, my gentle, peaceful, orderly, methodical father, has been indicted by the grand jury for mishandling bank funds."

"I'm so sorry, Colly. Surely they'll find that he didn't do it."

"I don't know. They've got a good case built up against him."

"Well, what does your father say? I mean, to you? What really happened?"

"I think Dad thought he was on sound ground, that he was doing what was best, but he took some risks and he let people who worked for him take some risks." He ran his hand across his forehead and she felt a twist of pain for him. She had always hated to see Colly hurt and she still did. She reached across the table to squeeze his hand.

"I'm sorry." Her hand closed over his. His head came up and his blue eyes nailed her. Her hand lying so still on his felt touched by fire, and she wanted to yank her fingers away.

His blue eyes were the sexiest she had ever seen. She couldn't get her breath, and all appetite had fled. Marilyn moved her hand away, feeling excited and young, feeling emotions she hadn't thought she ever would again.

"Ready to go?" he asked.

"Sure enough."

He took her arm and they walked to the door. She was suddenly aware of his height, of her head coming only to his shoulder. She waited while he paid the check, and then he held the door open for her.

"Where's your car?" he asked.

"It's the black one under the elm."

"Their lot is plenty big. Let's leave yours here and ride in mine. It's over there."

Two

He drove slowly, commenting on the changes in the
town as they headed back to an older part of the city.
Elms became taller, their long branches shading the
street. Sycamores with thick white trunks lined
blocks where two-story frame and red-brick houses
sat back from the street. Sidewalks were cracked,
angled upward by roots pushing through over the
years. Lawns were vivid green with pink, yellow, and
red spring flowers blooming in flower beds and
window boxes.

Marilyn felt as if she were drifting back in time.
Nostalgia assailed her, memories of lazy summer
days returning to fill her mind.

"Remember when we used to play under the sprin-
kler?" she asked.

"Yeah, when your mother didn't think it was
healthy under cold water when it was a hundred and
thirteen degrees in the shade."

"So you just squirted me with the hose, and I told her I couldn't help what you did."

He laughed. "I wonder how many things I got blamed for when I was perfectly innocent."

"You were never perfectly innocent, Colly!"

He pulled to the curb and climbed out in front of a neat red-brick colonial. A little girl sat on the porch swing and waved to them. "Hi."

Colly waved back. "Hi there."

He took Marilyn's hand. "Come on, Mit. Let's step through the Looking Glass."

"People live there."

"Sure they do. We'll tell them who we are."

The screen door opened and a young woman looked at them curiously. Colly turned on the charm as if he had thrown a switch. He flashed his dazzling smile, raised his voice to a polite level, and said, "Hello. This is Marilyn Pearson and I'm Colin Rankin. We grew up on this block, and this used to be my house."

"How nice." Smoothing auburn hair away from her face, the woman smiled and stepped onto the porch, letting the screen door swing shut behind her. "We bought the house from some people named Hadsen. I'm Rona Jakes and this is my daughter, Cara." The child moved close to her mother.

"Hi, Cara," Colly said, and winked. "We don't want to bother you. We just wanted to look at the yard and the block. Do the Bateses still live next door?"

"No. They moved away last year. The only people I know who have been here a long time are the Knudsons across the street."

"I'll be darned. Everyone's gone."

"Would you like to come in?"

"We don't want to be any trouble. Do you mind if we look at the backyard? There used to be a pear tree—"

"The pear tree! I love it. Come look at the house. Everything's a mess upstairs, but I don't mind if you don't."

They followed her inside, Cara trailing after them as they looked at the familiar rooms filled with unfamiliar furniture. Marilyn held Colly's hand and gazed at the old mahogany mantelpiece where she had helped him hang his Christmas stocking. They climbed the stairs to look at the room that used to sport model airplanes and wallpaper with brown bears, and later, football trophies and wallpaper with blue stripes. Now the walls were covered in pink and yellow flowers, and the room held white furniture and lots of dolls.

"This was my room," Colly said.

"It's mine now," Cara said shyly.

"It's a nice room. I liked to lie in bed listening to rain dripping off the roof and hitting the metal awning over the backdoor below."

"It makes a ping-ping sound."

"You listen to it too."

Cara nodded, looking pleased.

They went downstairs, and out through the kitchen where Marilyn had spent as many hours as she had in the kitchen of her own home. The old pear tree was taller now, its branches thicker and covered with green leaves. The Jakeses had stayed in the house, leaving Marilyn and Colly alone. They stood under the pear tree in silence until Marilyn asked, "Remember when you shot out the Hunts' windows with your new air rifle?"

He chuckled. "Yeah, but I didn't get caught. They

never did know what caused the glass to fall out of their kitchen window. Thank the Lord I didn't hurt anyone."

"You really were rotten sometimes."

"You weren't always an angel yourself." His blue eyes twinkled, and she felt a current spark the air between them.

"Is that so!"

"Yeah, that's so! You want to make something of it?"

She laughed. "You always won the shouting contests. Just because you were four years older. If we had been the same age, I could have held my own."

He reached up and pulled down a twig, sticking it into her thick, soft hair. "You could hold your own sometimes," he said in a deeper voice, turning strands of her hair over his fingers. Her breathing quickened as he continued, "I remember when you hid my baseball glove. You wouldn't admit you'd done it, but I knew you had."

"I did."

"Muzzy Mit! I knew you did! Dad bought me a new one, and I got a stern lecture about taking care of my things. Then, lo and behold, the old one suddenly appeared in the branches of the pear tree."

"I hid it beneath the front steps."

"I ought to get revenge."

She laughed. "Sorry. You can't now. When you cross the line of twenty-one years, everything that went before becomes null and void."

"Not everything," he said firmly in a tone of voice that made her heart flutter. He reached up into a fork in the branches of the tree, his white shirt stretching tautly across his broad shoulders. "Remember how we'd hide notes up here in the hollow part?"

"There won't be any there now."

"That's what you think," he said smugly, retrieving crumpled bits of yellow paper.

"Oh, Colly!" Her heart jumped as the papers stirred memories, and she moved closer to stand beside him as he tried to straighten them out without tearing them.

She looked at the crimped, blurred, and faded writing, recognizing her own note. "It's my writing."

Colly read it aloud, his bass voice soft and husky as they stood with arms touching. " 'I hate you Rotten Rankin! Your rotten rotten rotten!!! To the core. You'll be . . .' " He paused and squinted. "I can't read the next few words. ' . . . broke Ezmerelda's arm and Mom says she can't be fixed and now she only has one arm because . . .' "

"I remember," Marilyn said, looking up at him, noticing his strong jaw, the barely discernible dark stubble on his chin, the pulse beating in a vein in his throat, his gorgeous, thick-lashed eyes. "You broke my precious doll's arm off."

"Ezmerelda. I have a vague memory of you getting worked up over something I thought was a bunch of nonsense."

"Nonsense! Ezmerelda was my baby."

He smoothed the note and continued. " 'I hope your BB gun clogs with dirt. Stay away from my yard!' " He grinned at her then, and crinkles fanned from the corners of his eyes. She was standing close enough to detect an enticing scent on his skin. He turned his attention to the second note. "Maybe this is my reply." He smoothed it out and she saw it was in his big scrawl, shakier and more unreadable than now.

" 'Ezmerelda stinks! She is a sapy doll and you shouldn't hav tried to grab her when I was gonna fix her so it serves you right muzzy. I don't want in your yard aniway. and stay outta mine. i'll break her othher arm if you don't. i'm not as roten as you.' "

She laughed. "The spelling champ of Acorn Avenue!"

Colly grinned and ran his finger along her jaw. "I'm glad we made up."

"So am I." She felt breathless. He moved closer and his hand rested on her shoulder. Suddenly she wanted him to kiss her, she longed for him to lean down, and she wondered what it would be like to kiss him. The thought made her pulse drum, and she forgot that she was staring.

"Shall we go over to your house now?"

She nodded, unable to answer, and he took her hand again. How nicely it fit around hers, she mused, as they walked back to the kitchen door. They thanked Mrs. Jakes, said good-bye to Cara, and walked past the spirea hedge to the house next door.

"Oh, Colly, look!" She gazed at her old home, the two-story frame house. A "For Sale" sign was leaning against a mimosa in the front yard. White paint was peeling and the house was obviously vacant. Gone were the flower beds, the neatly trimmed lawn, the old rockers and the big white tubs of red geraniums on the porch.

"Colly, we shouldn't have come," she whispered, fighting back tears. "It looks terrible."

"Hey, Cinderella," he said gently. "Don't look at it as it is now. Let's remember what was here before."

She brushed away a tear and tried to imagine her house the way it used to be.

After they climbed up the steps, Colly picked the lock with ease.

"Sure you're in demolition and not breaking and entering?"

He grinned. "I learned to do that years ago. Mom would lock me out so that when I got home she could wake up and lecture me on the late hour. I used to pick the lock, tiptoe to bed, and that eliminated the lectures."

The door squeaked when he pushed it open. The house was dusty. Their footsteps made hollow sounds as they entered and stood in the wide hallway.

"Remember when I spilled the red paint on the stairs and your mother wasn't home?"

She smiled, suddenly feeling better. "We never scrubbed so hard and fast in our lives. I just knew it was the end of your life right then. You know how particular she was about everything."

"She took it pretty well, considering. I rather expected it to be the end of my life too."

"And remember when you hit me with a snowball and knocked out my front tooth and my dad came down to fuss at your dad and they got into a fight?"

Colly laughed, a hearty, inviting sound in the emptiness. "I thought I was a goner that time too—until our dads got into it. Mom was screaming and your mother fainted and the neighbors all came running. And I couldn't sit down for a week. I think the old man really gave it to me to get even for the bloody nose your dad gave him. All for one of your lousy front teeth!" He laughed again, and his merriment was contagious.

"You deserved it. I needed my front tooth."

"It was just a baby tooth."

"You got revenge, calling me Snaggle-Tooth for months. That embarrassed me."

"I would've gladly traded your embarrassment for the lickin' I got," he said with a flash of his white teeth. He brushed her shoulders, straightening her collar, then ran his knuckles over her collarbone. Streamers of heat radiated from his touch. "I wanted to punch out another tooth."

"You were so infuriating sometimes. I'd go from thinking you were my best friend on earth to hating you on sight. Maybe it's retribution for you to be missing a tooth now. Show me, Colly." She felt as exhilarated as if she were sledding downhill, going faster each second.

"And you show me your perfect teeth that are gorgeously straight and even and didn't get the tiniest crook from losing your little old baby tooth early."

"Braces straightened them out and you know it."

"Show me," he challenged.

"You show me first."

"Show me, Mit," he said softly, all teasing gone. She trembled slightly.

He leaned closer, smiling. Barely visible in the upper molars was a gap.

"It doesn't hurt your smile one iota," she said breathlessly. She could smell the musky scent of him again and she noticed how well shaped his lips were. She remembered looking at those lips a thousand times before, remembered their first kiss. She had taken weeks to come down to earth. A very simple kiss it had been, but at the time it had taken her from childhood into young womanhood.

His blue eyes were so very blue, she thought. He tilted her chin up and her heart beat ever faster. His breath fanned softly over her and his voice was deep.

"Remember that first kiss? You were the first girl."

"You were the first boy."

"Thanks for writing me that it wasn't such a bungled job," he drawled, and her heart lurched.

"It was marvelous," she whispered, and every inch of her being ached for Colly to pull her closer and repeat the kiss.

His arm slipped around her waist. "I can do better now."

"I can too."

"Show me."

"You show me first," she said, aware of the old childhood ritual that had never been said so breathlessly, never with such intensity. He pulled her closer and it was right, perfect. His hand held the back of her head.

She looked up at him, barely able to keep her eyes open while he studied her features with a slow thoroughness, as if memorizing each angle, each curve of bone and flesh.

"Mit, it's been such a long road," he said huskily. Then his lips brushed hers and she closed her eyes to a dizzying darkness.

His mouth settled firmly then and he did show her. It wasn't the same childish kiss at all. It was a man's kiss and an expert kiss. One that made her heart pound, her knees buckle, her body mold to his, and her arms tighten around his neck.

It was Colly and it was wonderful, she thought, the

most natural thing on earth. For a time she forgot everything—all her responsibilities, tomorrow or yesterday—just as he had said they would. She returned his kiss without thought of the consequences. But the result wasn't at all what she had expected.

She'd thought it would satisfy some deep need. Instead, though, it made her need mushroom and grow, as a brief remembrance of things past became suddenly important in the present.

Stunned, she looked up at him when he pulled his head away. They stared at each other, shaken by what had just taken place.

"Marilyn—"

She put her hand over his mouth. "Shh, Colly. We have just a few hours together. Just this afternoon. I can't look beyond that. You're leaving."

His blue eyes were dark as storm clouds, but he was silent, kissing the tips of her fingers lightly. He slipped his arm around her waist.

"Enough of the past. Come on. Let's go see the Ghost of Christmas Present."

She laughed. "Lewis Carroll, Grimms' Fairy Tales, and now Dickens. You don't care how you mix them, do you?"

He smiled and held her hand as they returned to the car. They drove away without looking back. She fought the lump in her throat until he pulled her against him.

"No sad moments today, Mit. I won't allow it. You know, I once punched Kevin Oakes in the nose for bragging that he had slept with you."

"Kevin Oakes!" She sat up and twisted around to

look at him. "That miserable jerk said that I slept with him?"

Colly laughed. "I didn't believe it."

"Oh, thanks a lot."

"Don't get in a huff. I just said I punched him in the nose for you."

"Well, I didn't know a thing about it."

"That's because I was such a knight in shining armor. Defender of a lady's honor without having to take credit for it, and all that."

She smiled then, and hugged him.

"Hey, save that hug for when I'm not driving. I'll go hit him again if I can have another hug."

She laughed and settled back in the seat. "You should have told me. Who else did you punch in the nose for me?"

"No one that I can recall. After I punched him, you see, the rumor was that *I* was sleeping with you."

"Colly!"

"Well, what would a bad mouth like Kevin Oates say when he got humiliated over a silly tenth-grade girl?"

"I see him in the grocery store about once a year, and he never speaks."

"Do you?"

"No, but I smile. After this, I won't smile."

He pulled her close. "Come sit by me, Muzzy."

"You know how I used to hate that name."

"Muzzy, Muzzy, Muzzy!"

"Rotten Rankin. Rotten Colly Corinthian Rankin."

"Enough!" He turned into a parking lot.

"This isn't The Corner. Where are you taking me?"

"I have some time before the witching hour when we must part. I want you to see my apartment."

Her heart jumped. Her brain told her she was act-ing in the most ridiculous fashion, but her heart skipped again and fluttered without paying any attention to reminders of good sense.

He climbed out and came around to open her door. She watched his long stride as he moved gracefully to her side.

"How did you grow up into such a man?"

"What do you mean?" he asked with great innocence.

"You know, broad shoulders, muscles, some sense."

"Same old Mit as always. The soul of compliments. Builder of egos."

"I think that was nice—broad shoulders, muscles, sense. Sexy blue eyes—"

"Now that's better. Definitely better." He led her along a path between landscaped beds of dwarf holly and purple hyacinths. They entered a wrought-iron gate where a fountain splashed with water in a tiny courtyard. Colly unlocked the door and held it open.

She entered a cool hallway, walking ahead of him into a living room that was slightly cluttered. Books and papers littered a desk, plants decorated a room that looked personal only because of the clutter. Marilyn gazed at it and felt a sudden pang, because she knew that if someone came through and picked up Colly's papers and books, the place would look as lived in as a motel room.

"This is nice."

"You don't approve."

"Sure I do." She turned and felt her breath stop. He stood in the doorway from the hall, leaning one hip against the jamb, one hand on his hip as he watched her. He straightened and came toward her, and her pounding pulse became a roar. His arms slipped around her waist.

"Colly, let's do be sensible."

"Of course," he drawled caressingly. "When haven't we been sensible?"

"How come we didn't have this effect on each other before now?"

"Beats me, but we sure as hell have it now, Mit." He leaned down to kiss her again, and it was even more devastating than before. And longer.

When he finally straightened, his breath was ragged.

"We've been together"—he paused and glanced at his watch—"three hours now. Not once in that time or in all your letters have you said anything about your present life."

"Colly, please, we agreed."

His eyes were solemn and searching. "How long have you been widowed?"

"Fourteen months."

"Is there a man now?"

"No."

"Do you know how right this is?"

She didn't have to ask what. He tilted her chin and leaned down, his lips covering hers as he kissed her hungrily and she responded. The next time they paused she was more breathless than ever. And just looking up into his heated blue eyes was as exciting as his kisses, she realized, stunned.

His hands brushed over her arms and up across her shoulders. "Mit, I can't keep my hands off you."

"I know," she answered as she kissed his throat, trailing her lips to his ear.

His hands moved like spring winds, warming,

caressing, touching one place lightly, then another, building a storm of passion that she was unable to contain.

His fingers drifted to her collar, releasing the top button on her blouse. He kissed her throat, moving lower over her collarbone, then down to the V of her blouse. His breath was hot on her skin as she wove her fingers through his thick, wavy hair, all of it precious to her because it was Colly.

He stood then and framed her face with his hands, holding her gently. His voice was raspy with desire and the look in his eyes was all-consuming.

"Mit, love, there's something between us that is long overdue."

Her mouth went dry and she couldn't make a sound. His hands stroked slowly down her back, then up to her nape, moving sensual, carrying a silent coaxing. Good sense never really had a chance. Marilyn loved Colly in a way she had never loved anyone else and never would love another.

"Don't say no," he urged in honeyed tones that fanned the flames in her heart into an inferno. "Dear Mit," he murmured, and the words were a caress that made her tremble. She was drowning in sensation. "Are you having an affair with the 'occasional guy' in your life?"

"No," she whispered, and shook her head, sure that Colly couldn't hear her answer.

"I didn't think you were. Let's take this afternoon. Just one time that has no strings, no ties except old memories. We're not strangers. We're closer than most lovers on this earth ever get to be. In all ways except one. Let's take this one time, a few hours, and share something good while we can. We can't change our lives. I know you have something that is holding you. You're tied up in knots. I can tell."

"Oh, Colly." She swayed, closing her eyes as she fought back tears.

"Mit." The word was husky. It was a question.

She opened her eyes and looked into his waiting ones. These few hours were a chance for something she'd never had before, a chance she might not ever have again, and she knew it.

She made a decision. There had been so few good times in the past few years, so many bad ones. Here was a chance for something to treasure. And she wouldn't get hurt. She stood on tiptoe, locked her arms around his neck, and raised her lips to his.

She saw the flare of satisfaction and joy in his eyes a moment before his arms crushed her and he leaned over her to kiss every concerned thought out of her mind.

His kisses obliterated the world. A hot longing spread through her loins and she thrust her hips against him, feeling his hard arousal.

"Oh, Colly! It's so good to be together," she whispered against his neck.

"It's going to be wonderful with us," he promised in a rasp.

She was with Colly, she told herself. It seemed right somehow. She felt loved and desired. And she could shut out the world, all demands and consequences. With Colly there wouldn't be any.

"Colly, I'm not protected."

"Shh, Mit. I'll handle it. You're safe with me."

Safe. She was safe. She was on fire. His hands left spirals of flame. Each touch, the slightest brush of his fingertips over her throat, her nape, made her gasp and moan with pleasure.

"Mit, what a fool I was. This is the way it should be . . . so right . . ."

"Colly, I may not be so good in bed—"

"Oh, Mit, if that isn't the biggest whopper you've ever told me!" he whispered as he kissed her throat, her neck, her tender nape.

She twisted her head so that he could reach her easily, her dark hair falling forward.

His hands were at the buttons of her blouse and, feeling yet another shock, she saw that he was trembling. She closed her hands over his.

"Colly, you're the dearest person I know!" she whispered, and kissed his knuckles. One hand was scarred, a jagged white line running from wristbone to the knuckle of his index finger. "You've been hurt."

"Yeah," he said hoarsely, and returned to the task of unbuttoning her blouse. He unfastened the buttons as he continued to kiss her. She felt the cool air on her flesh as he pushed away her blouse, then her bra and skirt. She stood there in a lacy white half-slip as he gazed at her lovingly, clasping her hips.

"Marilyn, how beautiful you are," he whispered, his big, tanned hands cupping her breasts.

Her hands were shaking as badly as his as she reached to unfasten his shirt, to peel it away and caress his hard, muscular chest, to wind her fingers in the short brown curls that covered his flesh, narrowing down to his flat stomach.

His thumb stroked across an eager peak and she moaned softly. His lips followed, his tongue touching so lightly, yet it made her gasp and quiver and ache for him.

He lifted her in his strong arms and carried her into the bedroom, to a big bed covered with dark blue sheets. A book was sent flying to the floor as he lowered her gently to the mattress. Then he peeled away the rest of his clothing, his eyes never leaving her.

She reached out, her fingers brushing his thigh as she gazed at him, wanting to remember forever her first sight of him. He was perfection, his magnificent body lean and fit and powerful. A strip of white flesh remained below his hips. He was aroused, aching with desire as she twisted, reaching for him.

He sat on the bed, pulling her into his arms, her midnight hair fanning over her shoulders as he whispered hoarsely, "You're my best friend on earth."

"And you're mine. Colly, it seems so perfect, so right."

He kissed her until she moaned and tried to move closer to him, running her fingers over his muscled back.

Colly gently pulled away the rest of her underclothes, tossing the filmy lace aside before he stretched out, fitting her to his length.

"Mit, what an idiot I was not to notice you before . . ."

"Shh, Colly."

He lowered himself between her legs, poising above her to look at her, his eyes heated with desire.

She slipped her hands around his narrow waist, looking up at him and relishing for a wild, hunger-filled moment that this was Colly, more special to her than anyone else. Eagerly she pulled him down to her. His maleness pressed into her softness, hot and hard, making her gasp.

He stopped and she moved wildly against him,

seeking release; he felt her need, willing her to greater urgency.

"Colly, please!"

He moved slowly, and she discovered an ecstasy beyond anything she had dreamed possible. She clung to his powerful strength, rising to meet each thrust, barely hearing his whispered endearments because of her roaring pulse. Need became all-consuming, burning through her as rapture spun a golden web around them.

"Mit! Oh, babe, how good!" Colly ground out the words and shuddered, sinking down heavily as he relaxed and stroked her, showering light kisses on her cheeks, her eyelids.

"Mit, I can't believe you're here in my arms. Feel our hearts. They're beating together."

She held him tightly, their legs entwined, as she whispered to him, intoxicated with the joy of it. "Colly, never before, never . . . hold me. Hold me closer."

Their words gradually faded and they lay still, locked in each other's arms. Colly rolled to his side and pulled her to him, her head on his chest, her soft hair spread over his arm.

"That was one of the most right things I've ever done in my whole life," he said, and her pulse thudded at his words.

"Colly, please don't bring in the outside world."

"I won't think of it if you don't want me to, but if you'll remember, I can keep a secret, and I have a large shoulder you can cry on." His hands moved down her back, over her buttocks, then up again, exploring as if he still couldn't get enough of her.

"How'd you get the scars on your hand and shoulder? I know about your knees and your shin."

"Demolition, my hand. Football, my shoulder and both knees. Falling out of the pear tree was how I hurt my shin."

"I remember. I was scared to death. Will Leah go to Dallas with you or stay here?"

"Leah who?" he asked in a bemused tone as he brushed damp strands of hair away from her face.

"Your secretary. I shouldn't have asked."

Blue eyes bored into her. "Ask any damn thing you want," he said in a harsh voice. "Leah and I'll part ways. It was most casual."

"Are you going to keep moving the rest of your life?"

"I don't know." He put his arm beneath his head and stared at the ceiling. "Sometimes I get sick of it. I'd like to have a home, but the business is good and I'd have to start over and I don't know what else I could do now."

She ran her fingers lightly over his marvelous chest, watching dark curls spring away. "You do have freckles—all over."

"Not quite," he drawled dryly, and she laughed.

"Have you worked at the restaurant long?"

"No."

"Sorry. Dammit, I keep forgetting to curb my tongue. I'm used to asking whatever I please with you."

"You still can," she said softly, kissing his shoulder, tasting his damp, salty flesh. "I just won't answer what I don't want to answer."

He caught her chin. His eyes searched hers. "Then what the hell is wrong in your life?"

She drew a deep breath, and for a moment she was

tempted to tell him everything, because Colly was the best friend she had ever had, but the afternoon had been perfect. She didn't want to spoil one minute of it by discussing the problems with her in-laws, and Jack's accident. She didn't want Colly's pity.

His voice dropped to the lowest pitch. "Forget that I asked. Go back to kissing my shoulder."

"Nothing big or dramatic. Just a lot of little things." She smiled briefly and did as he asked while he turned on his side to look at her. And then she was in his arms again and it was slower, better than before.

When they lay back satiated, exhausted, she said, "It's past dinnertime."

"How do you stay so trim eating the way you do?"

"I eat like a bird. And it was your stomach that protested just now, not mine."

"My stomach doesn't know a good deal when it sees one. I'm having fun. To hell with my stomach. Now, your stomach is another matter—a delightful one."

He leaned down to kiss her there, wavy locks of brown hair tumbling over his forehead, and she gasped. His words were muffled as he said, "Some bird—a vulture, maybe."

"Colly, you're asking for trouble," she replied, but there wasn't one shred of anger in her voice. His kisses trailed lower and she reached out to pull him to her. "Colly, you're a wonder."

"Think of all the time we wasted, sitting up in the treehouse reading comic books."

Her soft laughter faded as she kissed his throat, moving down across his chest. His breath was hissed as he wound his fingers in her hair. "I'll quit work and stay the rest of my life in bed if you will."

"Sure, Colly," she murmured between kisses. His flesh was warm, taut over muscles that were firm.

"I wish you meant that," he said gruffly, and she looked up in surprise because he sounded so solemn.

She turned away quickly, glancing down to run her finger over his hipbone. "How can a hipbone be so important, so sexy?"

"Because it is one of the two most beautiful hipbones in the world," he said, kissing the narrow indentation of her waist.

"You think you have beautiful hipbones?" she teased.

"You dope! Your hipbones, not mine. Mine are what I hang my pants on. Like a coat hanger."

"Sure, like a coat hanger. My heart doesn't jump and do sixty when I touch a coat hanger."

"That happens when you touch me?"

She looked up, and their bantering faded as he leaned over to kiss her again.

An hour later they went to eat dinner, driving to a large downtown hotel. After dinner they walked past small shops in the lobby until they reached a jewelry store.

"I need to get something for my mother. Want to help me select a gift? She's had a rough time as well as Dad."

Marilyn nodded and they entered the tiny jewelry store, walking on thick brown carpeting. Colly asked to see diamond drops, then diamond hearts. He fastened a heart with a thin golden chain around Marilyn's neck, his fingers brushing her flesh lightly, the necklace cold for a moment against her skin.

"Think she would like that?"

"Of course she would."

He unfastened it while the petite blond sales clerk smiled. "Now let's look at this." He put another thin gold chain, this time with a solitary diamond, around her neck.

Marilyn looked at it in the round mirror on the counter. The large diamond sparkled in the light and suddenly she felt better. Colly's business must be very good if he could casually walk in and buy his mother such a gift. She said, "It's lovely."

"Which one do you like best?"

"They're both beautiful."

"Mit, you're supposed to be a help."

"This one." She touched the glittering stone as she looked at her reflection in the mirror. She raised her eyes and her heart stopped at the expression in Colly's. It was both love and desire, a hunger so intense that it was breathtaking.

"I'll take this one. Can you gift wrap it?"

"Sure. Will there be anything else?"

"Yep." He looked around, pulled on Marilyn's arm, and moved down the counter. "Here are some pins. Pick one out, Mit. And before you fuss, these are inexpensive. Come on, indulge me."

She looked at the pins. None were the type of jewelry she wore. She studied a golden bee with red stones set in the wings, a gold four-leaf clover, and a small gold car.

"I'll take the four-leaf clover."

"Good."

"Anything else?"

Colly shook his head and followed the clerk to the register to pay for his purchases.

He carried the sack with the gift-wrapped box and the plain box, taking Mit's arm to walk to the car. "You can take me back to The Corner now to get my car."

"The night's young. Come home with me, Mit," he said, his voice becoming as thick and enticing as hot chocolate, stirring a responding heat that melted all her resistance.

Later, when she lay in his arms in his big bed, he stretched out a long bare arm, muscles flexing, as he reached to a bedside table to pick up the white sack. He shook out the gift-wrapped box and handed it to her.

"I bought you a present."

"Colly, this is your mother's!"

"It was never for one single second intended for my mother. Mom would take that straight to the safe-deposit box and never wear it. She'll love the pin you picked out. Open your present, Mit."

She tore the wrapping. "Colly, you shouldn't—"

"Oh, come on, don't start that. First present I've given you in years. I have all those Christmases to make up for."

She laughed as she peeled away the last of the paper. "The last present was that big stuffed bear you gave me for graduation."

"Do you still have bears on your bed?"

"No. Oh, Colly, this is so beautiful."

He grinned. "It's kind of a dirty trick. If you like the pin better, I'll get one tomorrow and send it to you."

She shook her head, looking at the stone glistening in her hand. Tears threatened, and there was a lump in her throat that prevented her from answering him. Colly was so dear, she thought tenderly, so special.

He tilted her face up. "Mit, I didn't give it to you to make you cry."

She flung her arms around his neck and clung tightly, her bare breasts pressed to his chest. Her voice was muffled against his shoulder. "Thank you, love. You're so wonderful."

He stroked her back and held her, and gradually his intent changed from comfort to arousal, banishing her sadness. She straightened to look at him.

"Put it on me, please."

His blue eyes darkened as he lifted the chain over her head. She bent her head to let him fasten the clasp. His fingers were feathery touches, his lips followed, and then she was wrapped in his arms again.

It was three A.M. when he drove her back to The Corner to pick up her car. As they sat in his car with the motor running, he said, "I'll follow you home and see you safely inside."

"I'm not going to invite you in, Colly. I have to go to work early in the morning and if you come in—"

"Shh. I know what you want, so stop fussing," he said in husky tones. He picked up her hand and looked at the Captain Flakey ring.

"You want to go to dinner tomorrow night?"

"Thank you, but I can't," she said in a rush, fighting the answer that sprang to her lips. She wanted to go with him more than she'd wanted anything in a long, long time, but she had to work. Before he could ask her for another time, she said, "We had an afternoon, Colly, a time for remembrance. I'll always treasure it, but we agreed today that it was just for a few hours when our paths crossed."

He gazed at her solemnly and her heart pounded.

"You're sure?"

She nodded, swallowing hard.

He reached into his pocket. "Here's my card with a phone number where you can reach me when I go to Dallas."

"If someone wants to hire you, how do they find you?"

"I have a headquarters in Denver, but I'm hardly ever there. The number's on my card. I usually go to the job, go bid on it. Mit, if you ever want me, just whistle. I'll come."

"Sure."

He pulled her into his arms and crushed her to him, kissing her hard. After a moment he whispered in her ear, "It's been so damned wonderful—sure it has to end?"

"I'm sure," she said swiftly, the hardest words she had said in her life. She climbed out quickly and reached to unlock the door to her car, but she couldn't see through a blur of tears.

His hand closed over hers, taking the keys from her hand. He unlocked the door, then straightened and pulled her into his arms. She clung tightly, trying to control her emotions.

"What is it, Mit?"

"I'm fine, Colly. Let's keep the day perfect. Please."

She felt his chest lift and fall as he took a deep breath and expelled it, but he remained quiet as she sat down in the car and closed the door.

He followed her home, waited in front of her apartment while she unlocked the door. She turned to wave, watching him drive away.

"Bye, Colly," she whispered, leaning her forehead

against the door as she closed it, remembering his touch, his deep laughter—

The phone rang. Marilyn stared at it, dreading any intrusion. She felt wrapped in a bubble of special joy, still surrounded with Colly's love.

The phone jangled again and, reluctantly, she picked up the receiver to hear the distraught voice of her mother-in-law.

Three

"Marilyn, where in heaven's name have you been? I've tried two hundred times to get you! Ralph's in the hospital. I don't know what will happen—" Gertie broke off, sobbing.

"Oh, no." Marilyn felt as if the bubble of warmth had burst and vanished, leaving her vulnerable to a chilling fear. "Gertie, are you at St. Mary's?"

"Yes, and I can't do anything for him. I need you—"

"I'll come right down. Are you in his room?"

"Yes. Please hurry."

"Gertie, don't cry. It won't help. Don't let Ralph hear you crying. What happened?"

"He doesn't know I'm crying. He fell and broke his hip. My back hurts now from sitting in this chair, and it's so cold in here."

"Ask the nurse for another blanket."

"Marilyn, please come down."

"I'll be right there."

She hung up the phone. "Welcome back to the real

world," she said aloud, her words a hollow echo in the silent apartment. She thought about her father-in-law, picturing his gray hair, his long thin face that was so unlike Jack's.

She showered, changed into a trim navy skirt and white blouse she could wear to work, then left for the hospital.

The corridors were silent, devoid of people except at the nurses' station. Marilyn stopped at the desk. "I'm Marilyn Pearson, Mr. Pearson's daughter-in-law. My mother-in-law just called me. Is there a nurse on duty I can talk to about his condition?"

A white-uniformed nurse crossed to where she stood and said, "Mr. Pearson is doing as well as can be expected. His hip was set this afternoon and he's sleeping now."

"What time will Dr. Baker be here in the morning?"

"Sometime between nine and eleven, probably."

"Could we have a cot sent to the room so my mother-in-law can sleep?"

"Yes, of course."

"And another blanket, please."

Squaring her shoulders, Marilyn went down the hall toward the room, bracing herself for an emotional scene with Gertie. Briefly, her fingers touched the diamond that lay under her blouse, the stone warm now from her skin.

As soon as she pushed open the door of the darkened room, a small woman stood up and began to cry. "Marilyn, thank goodness you're here!"

Marilyn crossed the room to hug her mother-in-law, then glanced at the man lying in the hospital bed.

"I'm having a cot sent in, and you can get some sleep."

"Will you watch Ralph?"

"Yes."

Within minutes a cot was delivered. Marilyn made it up and Gertie lay down on it, falling asleep swiftly. Marilyn sat in the chair, looking at the two people stretched out only a few feet away. She felt numb. Already the time with Colly was beginning to seem like a dream that hadn't really happened, something that would leave no imprint on her life. Except in her heart, she thought. She frowned in the darkness. Part of her heart would forever belong to Colin Rankin. She knew that now.

The next morning she hired a sitter for a few hours for her father-in-law, took Gertie home to rest, left a call for Dr. Baker's nurse so that she could find out about her father-in-law's prognosis, and went to work at the restaurant. She had a luncheon and a dinner to cater, and was too busy to think much about Colly.

Days ran together and Marilyn slipped back into her routine. Her father-in-law came home from the hospital, and Marilyn helped them find an aide to assist with his care. One afternoon at the end of June she arrived home from the restaurant and opened the mailbox. A large, black scrawl covered a fat envelope, and her heart jumped. She unlocked the door and stepped into the coolness of the hall, dropping her purse and ripping open the letter. Her hands shook as she found a piece of bubblegum inside and began to read.

June 27

Dear Mit:

I have a black hole in my heart, Mit. And I'm afraid it's going to suck the rest of my life down into it. So, I have to see you one more time. Don't make me wait five months this time to get a date. I'll be up for the holidays July 23, 24, and 25. Work me into that schedule of yours. I didn't see the inside of your apartment. I want to be able to picture it in my mind when we're apart. You can humor me that much.

Here's some bubblegum. I can remember how mad I'd get when you'd blow the biggest bubble. A twerpy girl four years younger and sixty pounds lighter blowing giant bubbles that topped mine! Can you still do it? I'm practicing, except that one popped at work the other day and three grown men hit the dust because they thought something had gone wrong with the explosives. Don't laugh, it was damned embarrassing. I just practice at night now. (Hampers my dating too. Grown women don't want to go out with men who blow giant bubbles.) Just kidding. I'm not dating anyone. Something happened to me in Oklahoma. My hormones changed. At a distance all the women in the world remind me of one person, and up close they turn into gray blobs that hold no interest for me. That's a scary thing to have happen to a red-blooded, healthy male. I had a physical. The doctor said I was fine except for things like my bum knees and my stress-sensitive stomach.

So, practice your bubbles and go out with me and we'll see who can blow the biggest one. If you beat me again, you've had it, Mit! I'll hold you down and get even. (Boy, oh boy, oh boy—I hope you beat me to pieces! I can't wait to get even.)

Dad's having a hell of a time. I wish I was working up there permanently. I think we have good lawyers. I hope so. I don't know what it'll do to my parents if he's found guilty. It's like a nightmare and I keep wanting to wake up.

Love and kisses (don't I wish!),
Colly

July 10

Dear Colly:

What holidays? We had an agreement and I think we should stick to it. A glimpse of the past is fun, but it's over. If you keep looking and looking at it, you lose all touch with reality. I live in a tiny apartment. Nothing special. Picture yours with ruffles.

Thanks for the bubblegum, but I don't chew anymore. I grew up and so did you. Keep on trying, the women will stop being gray blobs soon if you go out with them. There are some lovely ladies who will adore the socks off you. Anyone with your sexy charm and your red blood will recuperate from one brief afternoon of stepping into the past. Give it a try. What's the matter with your stomach? (It seemed great to me!)

Love,
Mit

She folded the letter, folded her arms, and put her head down to cry. She ached for Colly. She wanted his arms around her, his silly humor, his tenderness.

She looked at the letter, pulled out another piece of paper, and began to write.

July 10

Dear Colly:
What holiday? Don't you know we're playing with lighted matches again? One encore? How about dinner July 24? I'll take off from work.
I'm blowing bubbles right now. Giant bubbles. I'll beat you to pieces and laugh in your face. I can't wait for you to get even. Just try. Nyaa, nyaa, nyaa. So there, Rotten Rankin.
I love you,
Mit

She stared at the letter a long time, her hand on her forehead.
She turned around to look at her small apartment. It had always been a haven to her until her day with Colly. Now it seemed so empty. They both felt the same attraction, she thought. Her throat hurt as she looked down at the second letter. Carefully, she tore it to bits and threw it away.
Resolutely, she folded the first letter, tucked it inside an envelope, and addressed it. She mailed it the next morning on her way to work after a long, sleepless night.
She thought the aching need for Colly would diminish with time, but it grew worse.
A week later she opened the mailbox to find another envelope with the familiar scrawl. She dashed inside and sat down as she ripped open the envelope, letting it fall to the floor while she scanned his words.

July 16

Dear Mit:

Surprise, surprise. I'm in Chicago for two days to bid on a job, then back to Dallas. I'm sitting in the hotel looking out my window at the moon and thinking you are under the same moon and may be looking at it too. It makes you seem closer. What I'd really like, of course, is you right here in my lap.

Marilyn closed her eyes and held the paper to her heart, crushing the hotel stationery against her white blouse. "Colly, I miss you," she said to the empty room. She opened her eyes to read the rest of the letter.

The holiday I referred to didn't occur. It would have if you'd gone to dinner with me. But I don't give up easily. And while the past is over, we could have a future and a present. You're widowed. What is it, Mit? I don't have bacon rind on my hair now and I know how to kiss. (I think.) I didn't persist when we were together, but come on, tell your best friend what's going on in your life that keeps you so all-fired tied up?

Can I untie it and let you loose? I'm willing to give it a try. Come clean, Mit. Double-dare you. Double-quadruple-dare you!

How about Labor Day weekend? We could go to a lake and have fun . . . And I'll show you how my great(?) stomach reacts to stress.

Love and kisses and hugs,
Colly

She laughed and hugged the letter. The whole day was suddenly brighter. Chicago. Tonight she'd look at the moon and maybe it would make him seem closer.

She started to answer, then remembered she had to be at her night job earlier, so she tucked his letter in her pocket to answer later.

Later became days, and then, before she knew it, she opened the box to find another letter from him.

Marilyn sat down in the shade on the tiny porch of her apartment and opened his letter.

July 29

Mit:
You'll be sorry you didn't answer my letter. I'm writing you from the hospital in Dallas.

Her heart lurched and her eyes sped across his words:

I was inspecting an old apartment building, and some rotten flooring gave way and I fell through. Headline—Rotten Flooring Felled Rotten Rankin. I'll pause to wait for your laughter to die down. As you note, it's a brief pause.

I'll be home today. They just want me for observation. I now have a twisted ankle and bruises from head to toe, but all-in-all I feel lucky. Guess the old football days gave me good practice.

How about writing to a sick friend?

Is everything okay? If you need anything, let me know.

Love and kisses and hugs and a few gentle bites,
Colly

Marilyn folded the letter, changed to shorts and a T-shirt, drank a glass of iced tea, then drove to a nearby shop to hunt for an hour for just the right get-well card. As she walked in the door of her apartment, the phone was ringing. It was Gertie.

"Marilyn, can you come over? Dad fell again, and I've called an ambulance."

"I'll be right there."

She dropped the sack with the card for Colly and ran to change her clothes, aware she might be in for another long night at the hospital.

She came home, six hours later, after her father-in-law had been taken to the emergency room. They'd X-rayed him and checked him over, finally declaring that he had been merely bruised in the fall. Marilyn was exhausted and climbed into bed, forgetting all about the get-well card for Colly.

Four days later she found another envelope from Colly in the mailbox.

August 2

Dear Muzzy Mit:

You're on my blacklist. Some friend! No answer even when I fell through a floor. What do I have to do, fall off a roof?

I'm back in the hospital and know I can expect no sympathy from you. That apartment building is a jinx. I got into some poison oak while I was walking around the grounds, and you know my allergies. This is worse than the Christmas the folks got the Scotch pine, and that was pure hell. I have—good thing you're out of reach and I can't hear your laughter—hives. I'm twice my normal size and red. The freckles have been replaced by big red blotches. It's damned uncomfortable and boring to lie in a hospital bed. This is dullsville. Ugh. (Have I stirred a shred of sympathy yet?) I just pray Aunt Phoebe doesn't find out that I'm in Dallas. I'd be a captive audience here—the mere thought makes my stomach queasy.

Love and kisses and hugs and bites and caresses,
   Colly

Marilyn sat back and reread his letter. She envisioned Colly laid up in a hospital in Dallas where he didn't know a soul except an aunt he didn't want to see. She bit her lip. It had been bad enough to read that he had fallen through the floor; now this was more than she could bear.

She rinsed the dinner dishes, glanced several times at the letter, read it again, and finally picked up the phone and called the airlines.

It took only an hour to get to Dallas, and the fare was cheap, so she asked for time off from work and simply went to him.

Downstairs in the hospital she purchased a pot of purple mums. A nurse at the information desk gave her the number of Mr. Colin Rankin's room.

As she approached the partially open door, she heard voices. Feminine laughter rang out, and Marilyn stopped, staring in consternation at the door, suddenly feeling foolish for coming to see him. It was August, she reminded herself. He'd lived in Dallas since June. Colly didn't live in a vacuum, and he probably attracted women with the greatest of ease.

She heard them both laugh again.

"Are you looking for someone?" a nurse asked.

"No, thanks. There's the room I want."

Taking a deep breath, Marilyn stepped to the door and knocked.

"Come in," Colly called out. Her heart thudded against her rib cage when she stepped inside.

A nurse sat on the side of Colly's bed. She stood up instantly when Marilyn entered the room. Colly lay in bed glowering fiercely, his face red and blotchy. In the only chair in the room sat a large, buxom, gray-haired woman, but Marilyn barely noticed her.

"Mit!" Colly's features changed. Suddenly, Marilyn was glad she had come. All her doubts vanished when she heard the obvious welcome in Colly's voice. His blue eyes sparkled, making Marilyn warm with pleasure.

The nurse nodded to Marilyn as she left the room.

Without taking his eyes from Marilyn, Colly said, "Mit, you remember Aunt Phoebe. Aunt Phoebe, this is Marilyn Whitaker Pearson. Marilyn used to live on our—"

"Little Marilyn Whitaker. I know who she is, Colin. You were such a skinny little girl and you're so pretty now! And look at the lovely flowers you brought Colin. Isn't that nice! Of course, it was plants that put him in the hospital, so don't set them too close."

"It was poison oak, Aunt Phoebe. Those are mums."

"I know what they are, Colin. You shouldn't touch them in your condition."

"Yeah. How'd you get here, Mit?"

"I flew," Marilyn answered.

"My goodness," Aunt Phoebe said. "Your name's Pearson now. Are you married?"

"I'm widowed."

"How tragic. Is it recent?"

"A little over a year."

"You and Colin were childhood sweethearts, I thought. Are you Colin's girlfriend now?"

Marilyn opened her mouth to answer, but before she could, an emphatic low voice said, "Yes."

She raised her eyebrows as Colly glared at her intently.

"Isn't that nice! Colin, shame on you. Why didn't you tell me you had a girlfriend and that she's little Marilyn Whitaker! Isn't that lovely. Colin needs a woman. Which reminds me, Colin, on my way here, I went by your apartment to clean it."

Colly looked so shocked that Marilyn tried to hide her laughter by coughing. She held the mums in front of her and coughed violently, turning around to place them on a high shelf.

"How'd you get inside my apartment?"

"When I told your landlady who I was, she gave me a key."

"Hell's bells, anyone could get in."

"Don't swear, Colin. Of course they couldn't. The woman knew I was related to you. I told her all about our family."

Marilyn couldn't turn around. She fussed with the pot of flowers.

"Aunt Phoebe, my apartment is fine," he said grimly.

"It is now. I have your laundry in the car. I'll take it home to wash."

Marilyn had another coughing fit.

"You have a cold, Marilyn?" Aunt Phoebe asked.

Marilyn couldn't look at Colly. "No, ma'am. I just choked." She turned around at last and Colly was glowering at her, his brows drawn together in a scowl.

"When is the happy event? Are you two planning a wedding?" Aunt Phoebe asked.

Colly rolled his eyes, then closed them. "I feel faint."

"Good heavens!" Aunt Phoebe jumped up. "Should I call the nurse?"

"I think he'll be all right in a second," Marilyn said. "No, we don't have a date set."

"Do you have a ring?"

Marilyn shook her head.

"Then you're not officially engaged."

"Yes, we are," Colly said firmly. "Show her the diamond I gave you."

Marilyn produced her necklace, which was tucked inside the neckline of her dress. Aunt Phoebe came over to take a look at it.

"My, that's lovely. I'm surprised you could afford one that size, Colin."

"Marilyn's worth the sacrifice," he said dryly, and the lady in question smiled at him.

Aunt Phoebe sat back down.

"Come sit down, Mit." Colly patted the bed.

"Where did you go to college, Marilyn?"

"To the university."

"Do you work?"

Colly sat up straighter, and Marilyn could feel his eyes watching her.

"I'm a hostess at Hicks and I manage their catering service."

"I hope you don't have to do that all your life."

"It's a nice job," Marilyn said softly.

"Of course, once you and Colin are married, you'll start a family. Colin is getting too old to wait much longer."

"Aunt Phoebe—" he said with laughter in his voice.

"Well, it's true. And you ought to get out of that dreadful job you do. That's no way for a married man, much less a father, to live."

Marilyn looked down, smoothing her skirt over her knees.

"Since you're here, Marilyn, I'll run along home and do Colin's laundry. How long will you be here?"

Colly looked at her, waiting.

"My plane leaves at eleven o'clock tonight."

"Good, the family will get to see you. You've never met my daughter, Jewel's husband, Arthur, have you?"

"No, ma'am."

"Arthur is such a marvelous father. He's been so successful with his shoe stores. Have you heard of Perfection Shoe Stores?"

"I'm sorry, no."

"Well, that's too bad." Aunt Phoebe stood up, smoothing her pink and purple striped dress. "Come sit in the chair. I'm going home while you're here. We've tried to keep the poor boy company while he's laid up in the hospital from a job that no one should have to do."

Marilyn started to get up, but a strong hand closed around her wrist.

"Now, Colin, take your pills and don't do anything you shouldn't. I know what a stubborn little boy you used to be, and I doubt if you've completely outgrown it. Keep that hospital gown on. You'll take cold in this air conditioning otherwise."

"Bye, Aunt Phoebe."

"I'll see you later this afternoon. And this evening we'll be a few minutes so Marilyn can meet Arthur and see Jewel."

She left the room, closing the door behind her. Marilyn kept her head turned, trying to fight laughter, when suddenly a pillow hit her in the back of the head.

She grabbed it and burst into giggles.

"That damn woman—"

"Colly, shh! She might be able to hear you."

"She has driven me nuts!"

"Oh, Colin, don't be stubborn!"

"Dammit!" He yanked off the white hospital gown and threw it on the foot of the bed. "She made the nurse come in here and raised a ruckus until I put it on."

Marilyn covered her mouth with her hands and laughed.

"It's not funny! And she's invaded my apartment! I'll bet she burned the issue of *Playboy* I just bought. And that damned son-in-law of hers, Arthur. Old stuffed-shirt, holier-than-thou and better-than-thou Arthur. If he comes up here tonight and offers me a job again in one of his shoe stores, I will throw up on his two-tone wingtip shoes! Mit, let me out of bed."

She scooted off the side and went to sit in the chair while Colly hurried into the bathroom. She could hear him and realized he was being sick. When he came out, he looked pale everywhere he didn't have red splotches. A pair of dark brown pajama pants rode low on his trim hips and Marilyn drew her breath at the sight of him. Blotches and pale skin couldn't hide the hard muscles and appealing body.

"Should I call the nurse?" she asked, genuinely worried about him.

"No," he said gruffly as he climbed back into bed and pulled up the sheet. He lay back against the pillows and closed his eyes. "It'll pass in a minute."

"Is there something you can do for it?"

"Yeah, come sit here and let me hold your hand."

She moved to the bed again. "I don't think visitors or nurses are supposed to sit on the patient's bed."

He said a rude word and she laughed. "Colly, you look sick."

"I am. They're making me worse."

"Who? Aunt Phoebe made you sick?"

He kept his eyes closed. "In the years since we were kids, I've developed what my doctor calls a stressful stomach. I get sick when I'm under stress." He opened his eyes and looked at her. "And she is putting me under considerable stress."

"You threw up because of your aunt?"

"I do that, Mit, when I get upset." He sounded so pained and so accustomed to the condition that an idea dawned on her, and she asked him, "What else makes your stomach react?"

"Anything stressful," he said in a flat voice.

"Your job?"

"Yes, sometimes."

"Oh, Colly!"

"Hey." He opened his eyes and sat up. "It's not that bad."

"Can't you quit demolition and do something safe?"

"It's all I know. Mit, don't start on me. For the past

two hours, I've heard 'Eat your lettuce, Colin. Put on the hospital gown, Colin.' " Blue eyes leveled like two blue gun barrels. "If you laugh, I'll throttle you!"

"I won't laugh, but I'll bet your jaw stuck out six inches and smoke came out of your ears."

"My mother wrote her that I was in the hospital. I don't know why, but Mom has always had a blind side when it comes to that woman. They're not one bit alike. Aunt Phoebe hates Dad. If it weren't for Mom's feelings, and especially now, I'd tell Aunt Phoebe to go jump in the lake."

"No, you wouldn't."

"Yes, I would." He rubbed his shoulder. "I'm sorry she was here when you arrived."

"You shouldn't have told her I was your girlfriend."

"Huh! She told me Jewel would find one of her nice friends for me to date."

Marilyn laughed until his fingers closed over her hand. His voice lowered. "I'm so glad you came."

Her laughter vanished and she looked down at his blotchy fingers holding hers. "I'm glad I did too. Is there anything you can do for the hives?"

"Here, put a little of this ointment on me, will you?"

"Did you get my card?"

"Yeah. I'm sorry I wrote such nasty things about your ignoring me while I was in the hospital before."

"My card and your letter must have crossed in the mail."

"Mit, I don't want to share you with Aunt Phoebe and that family of hers. She'll be back again in about an hour, then they'll all come back at seven."

"Can't the nurse quarantine you?"

"No."

"Well, I can." Marilyn looked in her purse, pulled

out a note pad and pen, and wrote: "No Visitors Allowed—Staff Only." She stuck the sign on the outside of the door.

"The nurse will take that down or tell them the truth."

"Or leave it. Nurses are busy." She sat down on the bed again, her thigh touching his.

He laid his hand lightly on her knee. "How easy— you come in and get rid of the pests with no fanfare. Would you like a job?"

"Getting rid of pests?"

"Yep, and warming a cold heart."

"You don't have a cold heart!"

"Feel it and see," he coaxed in his rumbly voice that generated tingles. Solemnly he said, "What a time for you to come! I can't hug you or kiss you or"—his voice lowered—"undress you—"

"Colly!" she said, stopping him, but her pulse jumped. "I felt sorry for you, picturing you suffering all alone in the hospital. I didn't know you'd have your aunt and a nurse in here. Don't tell me that cute blond nurse is a pest."

He grinned. "Ginger? No, I'll take Ginger any day over Aunt Phoebe. Let me see your plane ticket."

She pulled it out and handed it to him. He glanced at it and tucked it under the sheet.

"Colly, don't become difficult."

"Stay until tomorrow, please. Just stay with me."

"Give me my ticket. I have to be at work in the morning."

"How early?"

"Eleven."

"You can get a flight back by eleven."

"Colly, don't be obstreperous."

"What's that? Come on, you're here. I'm sick and I need a friend. Call work and tell them your brother is sick and you have to take the morning off. Or get back by eleven." He rubbed his shoulder, then grimaced. "Let me call and change your ticket."

She looked into deep blue eyes that were the most wonderful eyes in the world. He was too sick to do anything that would entangle her deeply, she decided. How could she refuse? "All right, Colly."

He dialed, changed the flight time to eight in the morning, and hung up, smiling at her. "Thanks, Mit."

"It wasn't much—"

A knock interrupted them, and a doctor entered. He was laughing as he looked questioningly at Marilyn, who moved to the chair.

" 'Staff Only' allowed to see you?"

"Hank, this is Marilyn Pearson from Oklahoma. Marilyn, Dr. Hank Jackson, who also is from Oklahoma City and went to the university."

Marilyn smiled and started toward the door, but the doctor waved his hand.

"You don't need to leave."

The doctor looked at her with amusement and said, "You two needed privacy? I didn't know you were that well, Colly."

"Marilyn did it to rescue me from my aunt," Colly said, grinning while Marilyn blushed.

"Say no more." Dr. Jackson's brown eyes rested on Marilyn. "I was here yesterday when his aunt was visiting. We'll leave the sign alone."

"Better yet, let me go home. Marilyn will take care of me tonight."

Startled, Marilyn held her breath, waiting to see what the doctor decided.

He nodded. "All right. Home with you, but stay on the medication and come to my office in three days."

"Thanks."

An hour later, they entered Colly's darkened apartment. He switched on the light and started swearing. "Aunt Phoebe has moved all my things."

"We'll find everything. Come get into bed."

He closed his eyes and swore. "How I've dreamed of you saying that. Now, when you do, I'm red and blotchy and sick!"

She laughed. "Come on, Rotten. Grizzly would be more like it."

"Sorry." He squeezed her waist. "I've been a bear. It's just so great to have you here." Her heart jumped from the squeeze; she wouldn't tell him how great it was to be with him, just to look at him and talk to him.

Settling in bed, he leaned back against the pillows and closed his eyes. Within seconds he was asleep. Marilyn tiptoed out of the room and went to the kitchen. It was neat and bare, with so few groceries she wondered if Colly spent most of his time elsewhere or ate all his meals out.

When he opened his eyes, she was seated in a chair a few feet away from his bed.

"Some company I am, but I'm exhausted."

"Sleep away."

"You'll have to sleep on the sofa tonight."

"That's fine."

His blue eyes were steadfast on her and his voice was a warm rasp that caressed her like strokes from his fingers. "Hives aren't contagious, you know."

"Colly, no! Don't make it more difficult for me to get on the plane tomorrow. I came because you were sick."

He smiled and patted the bed. "Don't sit so far away."

The buzz of the doorbell interrupted them and he groaned. "That's Aunt Phoebe! I know it's her."

"Muzzy Mit to the rescue." Marilyn rose and left the room to return fifteen minutes later carrying an armload of laundry.

Colly sat up straighter. "I feel one hundred percent better already. How did you get rid of her?"

"I told her that you and I needed to be alone to plan our wedding in the short time I'm here."

"I'll be damned!"

Marilyn blushed. "Well, maybe it wasn't nice, but I didn't fly to Dallas to spend my time with Aunt Phoebe."

His grin widened. "Gee whiz, you're a wonder."

"Tell me where everything goes."

"Just toss it all on the dresser. I'll put it away later."

Marilyn looked down at the armload of clean laundry. "Including your bright red shorts?"

He laughed. "Probably made Aunt Phoebe faint. Now, put down the laundry and come back here beside me. Hold my hand."

She sat down on the side of the bed.

"Are you going to tell me yet what's going on in your life?"

"Not yet. You don't have anything to eat. I'll go to the grocery for you."

"Will you stop being practical for ten minutes and just let me touch you? You can't catch hives and I'm feeling better and better. Come a little closer, babe," he urged her softly.

"Colly, you know you should lie still and recuperate," she said, but it was difficult to ignore the broad, bare shoulders that she had dreamed of endless times since May. He pulled her to him and she couldn't resist.

"Don't . . . you'll get worse."

"Shh, hives don't get worse from kissing." His lips brushed hers briefly before she straightened. Her heartbeat fluttered and raced, but she said, "If you had to go back to the hospital because you didn't get enough rest at home, I'd feel terrible."

He groaned. "And I'm going to feel worse than terrible if I can't kiss you."

"One kiss."

"Sure enough, Mit," he said in his low, sexy voice that didn't have the tiniest thing wrong with it, a voice that sent ripples of heat down her spine.

"Oh, Colly, this is—" she whispered as his mouth met hers, stopping her words. She closed her eyes. Hives had nothing to do with kissing, she reminded herself. He was still the sexiest, best kisser on earth, and she placed her hands on either side of his hips on the bed, leaning closer to him as consciousness spun away on the winds of desire.

Finally she straightened and, as he reached for her again, she stood up. "We'd better stop," she said breathlessly.

"What's the matter with your voice?" he asked in a rasp.

"The same thing that's wrong with yours."

"Damn the hives and damn poison oak."

"Don't fuss. I wouldn't be here if it weren't for them."

"Then I love having the hives!"

She laughed, trying to fight the wild urge to sit back down on the bed with him and close her eyes again. "I'm going to the grocery. I'll be back soon."

"Don't you want a list?"

"I know what you like." She left, shopped for an hour, and returned to cook spaghetti for him. They sat and talked for hours. Finally, at midnight, she said, "I go to the sofa now. I know you're tired."

"Look in the dresser. You can wear my pajamas." He scooted over. "Mit, just lie down here and let me hold your hand."

"You're sick, I'm not. I couldn't take that."

"Go off to the sofa then. You'll miss me."

She showered, dressed in navy blue pajamas that hung over her hands and drooped over her shoulders. She rolled up the long legs and locked up the house, turning out most of the lights. Then she went into Colly's room.

He lay there half-sleeping, his chest rising and falling evenly. A soft light from the bathroom made angles and planes in his face dark and shadowy. She slipped beneath the cool sheets and reached over to take his hand, his warm fingers wrapping around hers. He turned to look at her, wrapping his arm around her. "This is one of the worst moments of my life—in bed with the most desirable woman on earth and all I can do is sleep!"

"Colly, stop. If you don't sleep, I'll have to go." She ached to pull his head closer and kiss him. Heat radiated from him, and every nerve in her body felt raw.

He closed his eyes and within seconds he was

asleep. She lay quietly looking at him in the dim light, memorizing each feature. Gently, she touched his cheek, and wound her fingers through his hair, thinking that the day had made the ties on her heart stronger. She loved Colly, she admitted at last, and she always would.

In the morning she tiptoed out while he was asleep, preferring to go rather than having to say good-bye. In an hour she was back home, ready to pick up her life where she had left it.

Two days later there was a letter in the mailbox. She ripped it open on the porch and sat down to read.

August 8

Muzzy:

You really were your muzziest to slip out of here without kissing me good-bye. Come back. I've broken out twice as much, sprained both ankles, and am twiddling my thumbs in boredom in my apartment. Here's a round-trip ticket for Sunday afternoon. Please. With sugar on it.

Hugs and kisses,
Colly

She stared at the letter, rereading it and turning the plane ticket in her hand. If he was so ill, how had he purchased the ticket? She had a suspicion that Rotten Rankin just wanted to spend Sunday afternoon with her, that he was perfectly well now. Her heart jumped at the thought of spending an afternoon with Colly if he were well.

She looked at the ticket again and sighed, then went inside to call his apartment.

No answer. She tapped the ticket on the table.

The next afternoon she wrote to Colly.

August 11

Dear Rotten Rankin:

Here is your round-trip ticket. You can get your money back. I called your apartment and you were OUT. Difficult to do with two sprained ankles and hives. I called your office and you were IN. Even more difficult to do. You can still be thoroughly Rotten. What a whopper!

Stay out of poison oak and off rotten floors and away from Aunt Phoebe and you'll get along fine.

Thanks anyway.

Love,

Mit

P.S. I'm glad you're well.

She mailed the letter, then checked the mailbox for the next week, but got no answer. The week became weeks and then September arrived with no more letters from Colly. And it hurt. She told herself that it was for the best and that the pain would diminish in time. Time always healed, she told herself. Or so she had thought, but it didn't. One day four weeks later, when she was finally finished at work and ready to leave, she thought about the mailbox at home and her step quickened.

She left the back door at Hicks, stepping into the tree-shaded parking lot. Indian summer days had set in—the leaves remained green, the air still warm.

Marilyn's red skirt swirled against her long legs as her high red sandals clicked on the asphalt. She snapped her purse shut and looked up, her gaze moving to the end of the lot, where she had parked her car beneath a tree. Her heart, her breath, and her legs stopped functioning as she stared at Colly.

He was leaning against her car, his arms folded across his chest, his eyes clear and deep blue, his jaw thrust out slightly. As she stared at him, he straightened and squared his shoulders.

Her heart resumed beating, skittering wildly.

"What are you doing here, Colly?"

"I had a little free time."

She felt a flush sweep over her and her cheeks became hot. She knew that look in his eye. She tried quickly to think what to do with him, how to keep him from stepping into her life and taking charge.

Four

"You should have let me know you were coming," she said, barely aware of her words.

"I thought I'd surprise you the way you did me. Come on, Mit. Let's go home," he said in his resonant, sexy voice.

He took her arm and led her around to the passenger side of the car. When she tried to hand him the keys her fingers were shaking. Without a word he let her in, then went around the car to the driver's seat.

"You haven't written in a while," she said stiffly. "I thought you'd moved on to another job, gotten too busy. . . ."

"You're right about the job. I'm working in Detroit now."

Her head whipped around. "You came down here from Detroit?"

"Dad's trial is coming up, remember?"

"Oh." She knew she ought to feel relieved that he

had come back to be with his parents, but she felt only a sharp twinge of disappointment.

"You haven't written either, Mit."

"No. Have you been all right? No more hives?"

"No hives. I've had a little bout with my stomach, though."

She glanced quickly at him and away. Her mind was racing. He looked tense, as if he were ready to tackle an unpleasant task. In her heart she knew why he was in Oklahoma, why he was driving her home in grim silence.

She twisted in the seat to face him. "Colly, we agreed on one afternoon."

"Yeah."

"You're breaking the agreement."

"Am I really?"

His carefully controlled, pleasant answers terrified her. She tried again. "Colly, my life is complicated enough. I have my defenses built against getting hurt badly. Don't tear them down. Don't leave me completely vulnerable."

He gazed straight ahead, watching the traffic, driving slightly over the speed limit. His voice remained so even that if she hadn't known him, she would have been fooled.

"Since you were ten years old and I stopped hitting you with mudballs and pushing you out of the swing, have I ever really hurt you?"

"No." She could barely murmur the answer.

He stopped in front of her apartment and came around to help her from the car. As if it were his house instead of hers, he unlocked the door and led her inside. Then he closed and leaned against the door.

She tried to think of something to say to ease the tension, to stop his steady, probing stare. "Would you like a cup of coffee?" Her gaze skittered away from the eyes that were two hot beams burning into her soul.

He caught her around the waist, pulling her close, tilting her head up. "Look at me, Mit," he said in his husky voice.

She did, and was lost. A sob was muffled in her throat by his mouth over hers. Desire burst through her like a bright hot flame. She was in Colly's arms at last, holding him, kissing him. What she had dreamed of over and over again was finally real.

Suddenly he stopped and cradled her face in his hands.

"Now, what the hell is going on in your life?"

"It's just a whole lot of little things. Ordinary, every-day responsibilities."

"Oh, yeah, sure, Muzzy. That's why you can't look at me and you have tears running down your cheeks. Tell me one of the little things."

She opened her eyes then and wiped her cheeks. "All right, Colly, I'll tell you about my life. Do you want to have coffee while we talk?"

"No, thanks. Tell me, Mit," he said, so gently she felt as if she had found shelter in a raging storm.

"Jack and I had a good marriage. He was the only child of doting parents. When he was grown, he was very successful, their golden boy who could do no wrong. They traveled with us occasionally and we saw them often. Jack was always there whenever they needed someone."

Colly frowned as he listened to her. His hands slipped down to her shoulders, running over her back with gentle strokes. She couldn't keep her hands from touching him and reached up to undo the top button of his white shirt, to smooth back the collar with care as she gazed at the strong, tanned column of his throat.

"We were close to his parents, especially after I lost mine. He was the sunshine in their lives, and when he died, they just transferred their attachment to me."

"So they like you. I love you."

"Colly!" She drew a deep breath. "You don't understand. They depend on me. I'm the only child they have now. The day you and I spent together last summer—when I got home that night, Gertie, my mother-in-law, had been calling again and again looking for me. My father-in-law had fallen and broken his hip. She was in tears. I went to the hospital—"

"It must have been after three o'clock in the morning."

"It was half past three. I got a cot for Gertie so she could sleep and I stayed there all night. The next day I arranged for a sitter. Gertie doesn't drive, and since Ralph fell, he hasn't driven."

"So you're tied to your in-laws. I have parents and I'm an only child, and it hasn't wrecked my life."

"You're not seeing this clearly. When I lost Jack, we just all clung together. They were my world, I was theirs. They need me. They depend on me. If you and I were really to plunge into a serious relationship—"

"Like marriage," he said, and his jaw thrust out a fraction more. She was stunned by his words. Her heart did loops, her stomach fluttered, and she felt a strange hurt inside.

"We've been together only a few hours—"

"And known each other a lifetime."

She frowned, finding it difficult to finish what she was saying. "If we had a serious relationship, and I abandoned them, what would they do when there's a crisis?"

"Mit, you're really muzzy sometimes. It doesn't sound like such a big deal to me. You have your own apartment. They don't depend on you totally."

"No, but I'm all the family they have left. Jack was ten years older than I, and his parents are much older than ours. They're sick often, and they need someone. They also need someone emotionally because it shattered them when Jack was killed."

"I can understand some of what you're telling me," he said gently. "Let's work on it, Mit," he went on. "Nothing drastic at first. Just let me into your life for more than an afternoon."

"Oh, Colly!" She looked away, not daring to gaze into his eyes and see what he was feeling. "That's what scares me so. Let you in just a little, and my heart is yours. Then if things don't work out, I can't—"

"I dare you," he said, so tenderly she felt the tears spring to her eyes.

"Colly, I can't turn my back on them."

"I didn't ask you to. Just let me into *your* life." His thumb grazed her cheek.

She knew if she said yes, disaster loomed. But she couldn't say no to the blue eyes that held such promises.

The silence was pervasive. She stroked his throat with her fingertips, feeling the strong, steady throb of his pulse. There was only one choice she could make.

"This will be worse than when you dared me to climb out the attic window."

His breath exhaled in a long hiss, and slowly a smile spread over his face, a smile that tugged the corners of his mouth upward, that crinkled the laugh lines at his eyes, that relaxed his features. "No, it won't," he said softly, his bass voice dropping with each word, lowering to that velvet depth that made her tremble in anticipation. "No broken arms this time. Now, what I've been dying to do since you walked out of that restaurant . . ." He crushed her to his chest and kissed her long and deeply, finally scooping her into his arms.

"Where's the bedroom?" he said against her lips.

"That way."

An hour later, she lay stretched out against him, trailing her fingers through the soft, curling hairs on his chest. "How long are you here for?"

"Until ten o'clock tonight."

She sat up, pushing her hair away from her face. "I thought you were here for the trial."

"Dad's trial—I still can't believe it—will be during the last week of November."

"You flew all the way from Detroit just for me?" She couldn't fight the grin that burst forth. "Colly, you're crazy!" Suddenly she frowned and sat up straighter. "Why didn't you write to me after you left?"

He twisted a lock of black hair around his finger, his knuckles brushing her bare skin. "You wouldn't go out with me or accept my invitation to Dallas." His blue eyes darkened and his voice lowered. "I tried to forget you, Mit. But I found out it was impossible, so here I am."

"Colly . . ." She leaned down to kiss him.

His arms tightened and she giggled.

"My kisses make you giggle, woman?"

She sat up then, her gaze trailing down the length of his tanned, muscular body. "When did you eat last? Your stomach is hungry."

He grinned. "It's been a while. I missed breakfast trying to get going early. I missed lunch. I had peanuts and soda on the plane. Let's go to dinner, then—"

"Colly, I work tonight." The glow of happiness diminished slightly, because she knew him well enough to see trouble ahead.

"You worked today. Don't they let you off after a shift?"

She stood up and gathered her clothes. "I'll call and see if I can find someone to take my place, but if I can't—you should've let me know you were coming."

"Yeah, sure. How come you work all day and all night?"

"Two jobs," she said, and ducked into the bathroom, locking the door and turning the taps on full.

Ten minutes later, she came out wrapped in a towel. "Your turn."

Without saying a word, he went to take his shower, but she knew what was on his mind. She dressed swiftly in jeans and a blue cotton shirt, then called to find someone to take her place. It took two calls, but she was able to trade nights with another hostess. When she replaced the receiver, she looked up to see Colly lounging in the bathroom doorway. Barechested and barefooted, with damp ringlets of brown hair curling over his ears, he had pulled on his slacks. He straightened and looked serious. "Tell me about your career."

"I know the look in your eyes. I told you there are just a lot of little things in my life. This is another."

As he sat on the side of the bed and pulled her down on his lap, her hands brushed his skin, warm and damp from the shower. His breath was fresh, tinted with traces of a mint toothpaste, and his eyes looked as determined as a charging bull's.

"So you work at Hicks in the daytime. Where do you work at night?"

"Jose's Chili House."

"Another restaurant. My, you're ambitious."

"Don't be sarcastic. It isn't like you."

"Then tell me the rest of the story."

"Don't you want to hear this over dinner?"

"No."

"You're getting a little—"

"Muzzy," he said in threatening tones. "Tell me right now."

She stared at him for a second, saw the futility of stalling, and said, "Jack was a very successful man. We lived in a lovely big house, took trips to Europe, even took his parents along a couple of times. Jack was willing to take risks, big risks in business, and he was lucky or right many times. He was a petroleum engineer, an independent oilman who invested heavily in wildcat rigs." Colly's attention was fully hers, but his fingers twisted a lock of her black hair as she talked, and sent dancing tingles down her spine with each light brush of his fingers.

"He made enough money to borrow enormous amounts. He had three businesses and several other ventures he invested in heavily. When his plane crashed, it was one of the times he was deeply in debt, and the businesses needed his management. Everything fell apart, and the debts were tremendous."

Colly swore softly. "So you're picking up the pieces."

"I'll have the last dime paid off at the end of this month and I can quit at Jose's. Now, I'm off tonight and your stomach is protesting violently."

"Wasn't there insurance?"

"No, Jack was always too busy, and besides, much of the time there was a lot of money available."

"You sold your house?"

"Yes."

"Where did you live?"

"On Chestnut Drive," she answered, realizing he would recognize the affluent area of town and know what type of home she'd had.

He wrapped his arms around her and pulled her to him. "Let me pay off this last month, and you quit tonight."

"Oh, no!" she said, touched that he would offer. "Thank you, Colly. You're sweet. Don't make me cry again."

"Who gets the money, the bank, a business?"

"None of your sly tricks, mister. You're not paying this off for me." She wriggled free and stood up. "Are you going to feed me or not?"

He stood to finish dressing. When they left, he draped his arm around her to walk to the car. It was dark outside, a cool fall evening with the leaves still green from summer. Colly pulled her closer and she slipped her arm around his waist. Their legs moved in unison and when he spoke, his voice was low and deep.

"Mit, do you support his parents? Do you need help there?"

She smiled. "No, thank heavens. They don't have any financial worries."

She almost lost her balance when he stopped abruptly. He dropped his hands to his hips and turned to face her, scowling.

"They don't *what*?"

"They don't have any financial worries, but they're not wealthy. They don't have the money Jack did. Colly, please, don't make an issue of it."

His eyes narrowed and he moved a step closer. "Let me get this straight. These dear little parents that are so dependent on you have let you work two jobs to pay off their son's debts."

"You're going to make an issue of it. Don't you want to eat first?"

"Do you have any excuse for their actions?"

"Yes," she said, beginning to get aggravated over his persistence. "They just don't realize what a burden this is."

Colly muttered a curse and threw up his hands, turning to walk away from her. She stared at his broad back until he turned around. Then she said, "They both worked hard to make a living and they're comfortable now. Jack was generous with them, and they put him on a pedestal. I didn't have the heart to tear him down in their eyes after he was gone. I consolidated things and sold the boat, the house, and his car, and got a second job."

"Couldn't they put two and two together?"

"No. They probably think I have plenty in the bank

because that's what they've done with their money. They don't spend it on themselves, they don't travel, they don't do anything. They both came out of poverty."

"And yet these two people who won't lift a finger to help you are taking all your time, attention, and care," he said, so bitterly she winced.

"I don't need the big house, and I like working at Hicks. I couldn't stay home and do nothing."

"Tell me how much you like working two jobs." He approached her again, his shoulders squared and his brows drawn together. "When we met that first afternoon, you were thinner and pale."

"At the time you said I looked nice."

"You looked better than nice," he said with sudden tenderness. They stared at each other without speaking. Then Colly smiled and said, "Come on, Mit. Let's go eat."

During dinner at a cozy Italian restaurant they talked only about safe topics, but as soon as they had finished, Colly leaned across the table. Flickering candlelight played over his features. "Are you going to take me to the airport?"

"Yes. Don't you want to call your folks?"

"I did before you got off work. Are there any other little ordinary difficulties in your life or do I have the whole picture now?"

"You have the whole picture."

"And we can't date because of the in-laws."

"Not at all, Colly. We'll date whenever you come to town."

"Good."

"But you know there's more to it than that. Earlier

today you mentioned marriage. Anything between us won't be casual. It can't be with me."

"You can't deny what we have. It's going to be permanent, Mit." Like glittering snowflakes, his words sparkled in the air, a tantalizing promise that she didn't feel free to accept. He trailed his fingers down her cheek and his words emerged in a tender rasp.

"Oh, Colly, please. We've spent so little time together. I can't think about a commitment. I can't leave them. Not yet. They're alone, and they've lost all they treasure most in the world."

"I'm not asking you to leave them. But I can't forgive that for fourteen months you've held two jobs, and they haven't given you a dime."

"I told you, they don't know. I haven't told them about the debts."

"Why the hell not? He was their son."

"The debts were mine and Jack's."

"*Yours* and Jack's?"

"I knew what he was doing. When they were obsessed with grief over losing him, I didn't want them to see what poor judgment he had used, what a muddle he had left behind. It would have been another cruel blow." She stared at the flickering flame, finding it easier to focus on than the angry look in his eyes. "Maybe it was emotional of me at the time and not the smartest thing to do, but it's done."

"But why in the world didn't they help you without your saying anything?"

"I told you, they probably think I have money in the bank."

After a moment's silence, he said, "Okay, I asked

you if we can date and you said yes. We'll go on from there."

She looked at him across the flame that turned his skin a coppery tint, noticing how the flickering light reflected in the depths of his eyes.

"Damn, it's time for me to get to the airport," he said. They left the restaurant, stepping out into a chillier night. At the airport they stood in a corner of the waiting area until his flight was called.

Colly held her shirt collar in his fingers, locks of her black hair curling over his wrists.

"You're letting them mess up your life, Mit."

"I hope not. But I won't abandon them."

He thrust out his hand and grasped hers. "How do you do, I'm not happy to meet Mit the Doormat."

She yanked her hand out of his, scowling at him. "That's not funny, Colly. I'm doing what I'd have wanted Jack to do. I can't help what his folks do."

"The hell with that. If they're financially comfortable and haven't helped you with their son's debts, why must you give up everything to become their keeper?"

"Because it's what I'd have wanted Jack to do if it had been the other way around," she said tiredly, her eyes closed. "Can we please change the subject?"

"No."

"You know, I'd forgotten how stubborn you are."

He leaned forward and held her shoulders. "You ain't seen nothin' yet, Muzzy. I'm going to ex-tri-cate you and extradite you out of working night and day if it takes my last breath."

"This is difficult enough, Colly, without you making it harder."

"They're adults. Would your folks have let Jack work two jobs to pay off your debts?"

She studied her hands. "How would I know?"

"You know damned well."

"Colly, you're tearing me in two."

A voice over the loudspeaker announced the last call for his flight to Detroit.

"Dammit, we can't part this way." He caught her to him, kissing her so hungrily that after the first stunned moment she forgot everyone in the room and simply wrapped her arms around his neck to return his kiss.

Finally he released her. "See you soon, Mit."

"Yeah, Colly."

His long legs strode off and in seconds he was gone.

She felt miserable as she watched the lights of his plane until they faded in the dark night. Then she returned to her apartment, trying to forget their dispute, remembering each precious moment he had been there. She went into the bathroom and stopped abruptly.

A box wrapped in white paper and tied in a blue ribbon rested on the edge of the sink. Laughing joyfully, she snatched it up, then sat down in the rocker, where she opened the gift carefully, wanting to save the bow and paper. Inside the box she found a small bottle of perfume. She recognized the bottle as containing the most expensive perfume on the market, but a new label had been pasted over the original. She held it up to look at the neat printing: "Midnight with the Camels." She turned the bottle in her hand. On the other side was another white label with Colly's careful printing: "I love you."

Smiling with all her heart, she hugged the bottle, then hurried to sit down and write to him.

October 4

Dear Colly:

Thank you, silly Colly Corinthian, for your version of Midnight with the Camels. Thank you more for the "I love you." It's mutual, you know.

Please try to understand my situation. It helped to have someone to talk to about my life. (Even if my listener was terribly cantankerous!) There's really been no one to talk to for so long. I traveled with Jack, and after he died, I just worked constantly. I don't have any close friends I feel free to unburden myself to. You're the closest, dear heart.

Watch out for falling bricks and poison oak. I'm glad I don't have to watch you work. It was bad enough when I used to have to watch you climb to the top of our elm or jump from your rooftop to the Bateses' roof. I'll bet you didn't know it made my heart stop. I'll bet you didn't know I thought you were the Acorn Avenue Superman. I really had a crush on you the year I was twelve and you were a handsome, dashing sixteen. Little did I know that it would be nothing compared to what I'm feeling now.

That's why I used to like to ride with you when you were learning how to drive. You know, I put my mother up to talking your mother into letting you drive me to my piano lessons. Take care of yourself. I love you.

    Mit

She folded the letter and propped it where she could look at it when she climbed into bed, into the bed she had shared with him earlier that afternoon.

She ran her fingers over the pillow, remembering, aching with longing.

The next day she mailed her letter. A week later, on Friday, she found one in her mailbox. Flinging off her sweater, she went inside to read it.

October 10

Dear Muzzy:

Want to come out and play? I'll be nice, I promise. You said we could date, so let's do. How about October 19? Let me meet the folks. I'll take everyone out to dinner.

No, I didn't know it made your heart stop to watch, but at the time I hoped it would. You made a good audience with your big green eyes. I think I may have been a little bit of a show-off.

So at last the truth comes out! I never could understand why my mother was so determined that I drive you to your piano lessons. I'll have to admit I was at a very dense age. I was put out with you and bored with the whole arrangement—which goes to show how flaky I was at that time. I'll drive you to your piano lessons now. (I learned to drive when I was fourteen, you know. It just wasn't legal.)

Mit, love, I think I was thoroughly Rotten Rankin when we were together, except in bed. I don't think I was R.R. then. I'll work on understanding.

I didn't take your advice and I was hit by a brick today (no kidding). I'm all right, but my arm is sore. My mind had wandered and I wasn't watching what I was doing. Guess where my mind had wandered? Mit, my life is so damned empty without you. This is the pits. Let me meet the Pearsons. I'll be on my best behavior—no skunk's tail in my pocket, no bacon rind on my hair—and maybe we'll all be one big, happy family.

I'm glad you can talk to me. And vice versa. Muzzy, you're my best friend in every way. Even when you're being your muzziest. Whatever happened to Ezmerelda? Do you still have her? I'll bet her arm is fine now.

I don't want to stop writing because it's a tie to you, but I have to go. When I think of you working two jobs I could tear down the buildings with my bare hands. The offer stands. I would be delighted to finish off the payments.

Love and kisses and get dinner set for the nineteenth.

Colly

Marilyn put down the letter and stared into space, worrying over how badly Colly had been hurt by the brick, and how to break the news to Gertie and Ralph that there was a new man in her life. She put away groceries and drove to the single-story red-brick home where her in-laws lived.

Gertie beamed when Marilyn entered the roomy kitchen. Late afternoon sunshine was pouring through the bay window on the west, glistening on the glossy red and white floor. Gertie closed the oak door of the pantry and turned around. "You're just in time for dinner."

"I can't stay long."

"You can eat. Just sit down there."

"How's Ralph?"

"His hip has hurt him more than usual today.

Maybe it's the cool weather. He's watching the five o'clock news."

"I'll go say hello to him." Marilyn found her father-in-law dozing in front of the television so she returned to the kitchen to help set the table.

"How was work today?"

"Fine."

"I've cooked the beans for three hours. Don't they smell good?"

Gertie lifted the lid of a steaming kettle, and the aroma of ham and beans filled the kitchen.

"Mmm, it does. Gertie, I have an old friend who wants to take us all to dinner Friday night."

Gertie stopped stirring, her hazel eyes round with curiosity. "You have a friend who wants to meet us?" Gertie blinked again and began stirring the beans vigorously. "A friend? A boyfriend?"

"We grew up together. He lived next door. We're old friends."

"Where's he live now?"

"In Denver."

"Colorado?" Gertie's voice wavered and she looked inquisitively at Marilyn. "When did you start dating if he's in Colorado?"

"He was here to visit his parents. He's here occasionally. We don't exactly date."

"Oh, I see."

"Will you and Ralph go to dinner with us?"

"I don't know why." She looked at Marilyn. "Are you getting married?"

"Gertie, he's only been here twice." Marilyn smiled, feeling something hurt inside. It was turning out to be more difficult than she'd thought it would be to tell

Gertie about Colly. She could see the fear and worry in Gertie's expression.

"Well, then, why does he want to take us out?"

"He knows you're my family now. He grew up living half the time in my house with my parents. Please, go with us."

"Well, it's ridiculous to spend so much money. We'll eat here."

"He'll want to take us out."

"No, you bring your young man here to meet us."

Marilyn hugged Gertie. "Thanks. I'll try to get off work early and help with dinner."

"You're a good girl, Marilyn." She patted Marilyn's arm. "Wait a minute. I have something to give you."

Gertie left the room and came back with a white box. "I found this today. I knew you'd want it."

Marilyn took the box and opened it to find a plaque, an award to Jack from the chamber of commerce for Outstanding Young Man of the Year. There were old snapshots of Jack receiving the award and a yellowed news clipping about it.

"Thanks, Gertie," Marilyn said, and closed the box, wondering if Gertie had intended all along to give it to her or if she had deliberately done so now to remind her of her ties to them. She took the box out to the car, breathing deeply in the crisp air. She looked back at the house and felt bound to its occupants by invisible ties that held her as tightly as heavy chains.

When she got home that night, she wrote to Colly.

October 13

Dear Colly:
Just a note so I can get this in the mail tonight.

I called information to get your number and they don't have a listing. Are you hiding from me?

We're set for Friday, October 19. I hope you get this in time. Let me know when you're arriving and I'll meet you at the airport. I hope you like the Pearsons. How could anyone resist you?

Thanks again for your offer to help, but with only a month to go until I can quit the night job, it's not necessary.

Mom gave Ezmerelda to my cousin Lurlene who lives in Tulsa. Remember Lurlene? She's the one who had such a crush on you (good taste, eh?) she'd take a book and sit on the fence to read, hoping you'd come talk to her. (Don't get any ideas, Buster. She's married and the mother of three now.)

And you didn't learn to drive when you were fourteen. You just drove—right over our iris bed. Or did you wipe that out of your memory too? Now that I look back, I recall that you taught me to drive—remember? That summer when you were home from college, and I was fifteen. Remember how you'd drive until we were out of sight of my house, then you'd let me take over? And when I hit the sweet gum tree, you took the blame. You had your good moments, kid.

I'd forgotten all about learning to drive. I was going steady with Kent Holloway that summer, and I loved to make him jealous by telling him about riding around with you. Dad thought I was the most remarkable pupil when he started to teach me to drive. It's funny that I had forgotten all about that. I suppose my mind was on Kent Holloway. I had some goofy lapses too.

See you the nineteenth, I hope.
Love,
Mit

She mailed it that night. When she came home from work the following evening, she opened the mailbox to find another letter from Colly. A gust of wind caught yellow leaves and swirled them against her ankles, sending them dancing down the walk. Marilyn tore the letter open. She unfolded white paper to read a big scrawl.

October 12

Dear Mit:
Will you marry me?
Colly

Her heart fluttered and skipped as much as the leaves in the wind. She read the lines again and again. Marry Colly. She closed her eyes and hugged the letter to her. A minute later she heard a voice at the curb say, "Ma'am?"

She turned around to see a man standing beside a parked car. He looked at her with curiosity.

"Are you all right?" he asked.

"Oh, yes, I'm fine. Thanks." Embarrassed, she went inside, where she leaned against the door and read Colly's letter again. Marry Colly. Her heart shouted yes while her mind kept racing over the complications. What would she do about Gertie and Ralph? If she traveled with Colly, she would have to leave them, and she didn't know how she could do it.

When the phone rang, she jumped.

"Mit?" The single syllable was a soft purr, a sensual, invisible caress.

"I just got your letter," she said breathlessly, her voice lowering.

"I like the way you said that. Your voice changed. You give me an answer Friday. I can't take one long distance."

"I wrote to you."

"You wrote an answer to my—"

"Oh, no! To your first letter about dinner on the nineteenth." She pulled out a chair and sat down, holding his letter to her chest. "We're set for Friday night. Gertie wants to cook so we're eating at their house."

"Hey, I'd like to take everyone out."

"I know, but she's happier cooking. She can't understand people spending money to eat out."

"Your voice has changed again. I detect a note of worry. Was it hard to tell her about me?"

"Yes."

"Be brave, Muzzy. It's for a good cause."

"I wrote you a long letter and mailed it last night."

"I can't wait." His voice dropped again to a deep, sexy timbre that reached out to her over the phone, making her temperature rise. "I can't wait to see you, to hold you."

She closed her eyes to listen, conjuring up a picture of him in her mind.

"I'm working nights now too," he said.

"How come?"

"To finish this job. The city wants the buildings down and cleared as soon as possible and are willing to pay overtime. When I'm not out working, I do the paperwork. I'm trying to finish and get home for

Dad's trial in November. Mit, I'd like for us to eat dinner with my folks soon."

"I'd love to see them again."

"They'd love to see you too."

"I hope so. Colly, I have to run."

"Job number two?"

"Yes."

"My plane arrives ten minutes after five Friday afternoon. I'll rent a car to get to your apartment."

"No, I can meet you."

"I won't argue with that." His voice became tender. "I love you, Mit." He hung up the phone and she squeezed the receiver. "I love you too, Colly," she whispered. She stared at his letter and began counting the hours until Colly would arrive.

Five

Eagerness kept her from sitting down to wait for his plane. She stood behind the thick plate-glass window and watched the jet come in and slow the runway, turning toward the terminal. Adjusting the coat over her arm, she glanced down again at her pale blue sweater over a white blouse, the matching blue skirt, her high-heeled navy pumps. As the passengers poured out, her heart drummed to a quickened beat.

Colly came off the plane in a rush, and the sight of him took her breath away. He looked so handsome, she thought lovingly. His skin was darker than ever, his hair slightly tousled. He wore a navy suit, white shirt, and conservative striped tie, and he looked marvelous and fit enough to be a male model. His eyes lit up with pleasure when he saw her. When he reached her he caught her arm and hurried her out of the crowd. As they walked down the wide hall, he stepped into the entryway leading to the visitors' observation tower. "Come here. I want to see something."

He dropped two dimes in the coin box, pushed the turnstile, and they climbed a flight of steps to an empty, round observation room where people could have a full view of the runways. Late afternoon sun splashed a golden glow over the room and its red carpet.

"Colly, what are you doing?" she asked with laughter in her voice.

He turned to hold her at arm's length. "I have to make an observation."

And he did, slowly, so slowly that every nerve in her body came alive. She tingled from head to toe as his appraisal inched downward over her sweater and skirt, over her long legs, then up again. He dropped his bag and pulled her into his arms to kiss her.

"Mit, marry me."

"Oh, Colly, I want to, but—"

"Shh. Engaged? How's engaged? One step at a time." He whispered against her lips, showering little hungry kisses on her. "I can't get enough of you. Oh, Mit." He pulled away and her heart pounded as she saw him reach into his pocket. He pulled out a small present, then tilted her head up to look into her eyes. His blue eyes were dark with desire and love, and she wanted to melt into his arms again, but she patiently waited.

He handed her the box and she opened it in silence, her fingers shaking. It was a ring box. As she raised the lid, his hands closed over hers.

"Give me your hand, Mit," he said in his huskiest voice.

Her pulse became an ocean's roar as she held out

her hand. His warm fingers closed over hers. "Let's get engaged."

She nodded, reaching up to touch his cheek tenderly. She watched as he removed Jack's rings and slipped a sparkling diamond on her finger.

She didn't know who made the first move then, but suddenly she was in his arms again, returning kisses that made the world go away completely.

The first moment she realized they weren't alone was when a giggle penetrated her consciousness. Then she heard voices. She started to pull away, but Colly's hands tightened, his kiss became even more fiery, and she forgot everything again. Seconds later, though, her eyes flew open and she saw people in her peripheral vision. She pulled away a fraction, feeling the heat flood her cheeks.

"Colly!"

Five people stood at the windows, three teenage girls and two adults. The girls watched the embracing couple gleefully while the adults stared out the window. When the man turned to look at them curiously, Colly grinned.

"We just got engaged." He tightened his arms around her waist, amusement and a gleam in his eye.

"Colly!" Wriggling free, she grabbed his hand to rush down the steps away from the onlookers. At the bottom of the stairs she slowed down to laugh breathlessly.

"You're Rotten Rankin, Colly, through and through. You embarrassed me."

He lifted long strands of her black hair and let them slide through his fingers. "I can't keep my hands off you, lovely lady. Let's get through dinner and go home."

Her breathing stopped and she ached to hold him, but she didn't want to make another scene in front of strangers.

"Let's go before we're late."

Colly drove the car while she sat next to him and admired her ring. "This is beautiful."

"I'm glad you like it."

"How's your arm?"

"It's okay."

She thought about Gertie and Ralph and her new ring. The first real twinge of worry came. "Colly, I want to wear Jack's rings to dinner. I'd like to break our relationship to them a little more gently."

"Sure, Mit."

"My, you're on your best behavior."

"That's 'cause I'm out with my best girl."

"Best? I better be your only girl."

"Don't worry. Would you believe that every attractive woman in Detroit, Michigan, still looks like you until she gets a foot away?"

"Maybe you were girl-watching when you got hit by a brick."

"No, I was Mit-remembering. Scoot closer to me."

"Your attention won't stay on your driving."

"Sure as hell won't," he said smugly, and she moved over to wrap her arm around his waist.

"I hope you like the Pearsons."

"I'll love anyone you love," he said lightly, but she wondered if it would be that simple.

"I didn't know your cousin Lurlene had a crush on me. I thought she was just really goofy for sitting on that uncomfortable fence in the hot sun to read a book."

Marilyn laughed, enjoying hearing the rumble in

his chest when he talked, loving the fresh smell of him.

"Who'd she marry?"

"T. A. Chesterfield. They live in Tulsa. Why?"

"Just curious."

She straightened. "There's the house, the red-brick one."

"What did the Pearsons do when they worked?"

"Gertie worked in a bank and Ralph was a pharmacist."

"How could she work all those years without learning to drive?" Colly swung into the narrow driveway and stopped the car.

"Ralph drove her to work. Sometimes a friend carpooled with her."

He shook his head. "And both businesses gave them retirement and pensions and benefits. Do you have hospitalization?"

"No. I plan on getting some as soon as I get the debt paid. You sound like an insurance salesman."

He didn't answer, but just came around to hold the door for her. She felt an attack of nerves. "How's your stomach?"

"Mine's okay. How's yours?"

"Suffering."

"Mit, I promise I'll put on my party manners. I won't throw food or juggle the dishes or—"

She laughed, relaxing a little. Then she asked, "Remember when we were little kids, how you'd toss scraps of food at me when your mother's back was turned?"

He chuckled. "You'd toss them right back."

"Your aim was better."

"Mom thought I was such a messy eater because all

the stuff you threw missed me and landed on the floor."

"Until she caught us."

"Yeah, that put an end to the food fights," he said, so wistfully she laughed again, and relaxed another fraction. "Your hands are like ice," he murmured.

The back door opened then, and Ralph stood there leaning on a cane. When he stepped back, Marilyn and Colly entered a small utility room.

"Ralph, this is Colin Rankin. Colin, this is my father-in-law, Ralph Pearson."

"Glad to meet you," Ralph said, shaking hands with Colly. "Mother's in the kitchen. Come in and let me take your coats."

The warmth of the brightly lit kitchen enveloped them, the aroma of fried chicken and hot coffee filling the air. Gertie stood at the stove tending potatoes boiling in a steaming kettle, tendrils of gray hair hanging in her eyes. She wore a red apron over her navy dress, and little beads of perspiration dotted her brow. At the sight of them, she dropped the lid on the kettle.

"Gertie, this is Colin Rankin. Colin, this is my mother-in-law, Gertie Pearson."

"How do you do, Mrs. Pearson."

"Fine. You two go have a seat with Dad and I'll be in shortly."

They moved through the house to the living room and Marilyn hung their coats in the front closet.

Ralph stood in the doorway. "Can I get you a drink?"

"No, thanks," Colly declined.

"Sit down, Colly." Marilyn waved her hand toward the green sofa. "I'll go help Gertie."

Within twenty minutes they were sitting down at the oval dining room table. As the platter of chicken was passed, Gertie said, "Did you know our son Jack, Mr. Rankin?"

"Just call me Colin. No, I didn't."

"After dinner, I'll show you his picture. He and Marilyn had so many pictures together."

Marilyn began to get a cold knot in her stomach. She looked across the table at Colly, and he winked.

"What business are you in?" Mr. Pearson asked.

"Demolition."

"Isn't that terribly dangerous?" Gertie asked.

"We try to be careful."

"My goodness, I'd worry constantly if Ralph did that. Have you ever been hurt?"

"Once or twice." He smiled. "Nothing serious. The chicken is delicious."

"Thank you. It was always Jack's favorite."

"What did you study in college?" Ralph asked.

"I majored in finance. And I played football."

"And then he went on to the pros," Marilyn said. "Are you going to watch the game this Saturday afternoon?" she asked Ralph, trying to turn the conversation to more neutral ground. For a moment the two men discussed the coming clash of the two state university teams.

When there was a lull Gertie spoke up. "Our son played football in college. He won that fancy trophy they give the outstanding player of the year."

Colly raised his eyebrows, surprise in his expression. "Jack Pearson. He went to Texas to school, didn't he?" asked Colly, and looked at Marilyn.

"Yes."

"I remember seeing him play once."

"The pros wanted him," Gertie continued. "He was torn between that or a career, and the career won. You know, he was a millionaire by the time he was thirty."

Colly's fork clinked in his plate and Marilyn glimpsed a flash of anger before she too looked down at her plate. Her hands were icy. She said, "Gertie, Windham's is having a shoe sale Saturday. I'll take you to get some new shoes."

"Fine. Where's your home, Mr. Rankin?"

"In Denver."

"Oh. Do you have relatives there?"

"No. My parents live here."

Marilyn was struck by an icy chill that made her shiver. She hadn't remembered to tell Gertie and Ralph about Colly's father. She drew a deep breath, wracking her mind for an innocuous topic.

"Rankin," Gertie said. "There's a Rankin who's in trouble with the law because he took the Sterling Bank's money."

"Gertie, that's Colly's father, but he didn't take the bank's money." Marilyn watched Colly carefully cut into his piece of chicken.

"Oh, my. I'm terribly sorry." Gertie blushed.

"That's all right," Colly said in his quiet, polite voice, and Marilyn felt worse than ever.

"I just was going on what I read in the papers," Gertie added. Marilyn had lost her appetite, and began to wonder how she would get through one of Gertie's heavy desserts.

"How did you two get started dating?"

"I saw her picture in the paper when I was here on a job," Colly answered.

"Oh, you were living here?"

"For a short time this year. I demolished the Canton Building."

"Lordy, why?" Ralph said, peering through his glasses at Colly. Marilyn wanted to throw up her hands, scream, and go home. The Pearsons were behaving badly, but she knew they felt threatened by Colly. She ached for them and she ached for Colly too.

"I was hired to do it," Colly said as politely as ever.

"Well, they're tearing everything good down and building flimsy stuff that won't be here a hundred years from now. Doesn't it just hurt you to destroy something so solid and fine and historical?"

"Ralph, it's his work," Marilyn said.

"And that's how I try to view it, sir," Colly answered. "It's a job. Someone has to do it."

"Humpf. Glad it isn't me. Jack fought the destruction of the old Panel Library on Fifth, and he won. He's the one who had this neighborhood declared an historical preservation area. No one's gonna tear it down ever."

"Now, that's real fine, sir," Colly said.

"And you own a home in Denver?" Gertie asked.

"Yes, ma'am. When I'm working I rent a small apartment like Marilyn does." Marilyn caught another flash of fire in his eyes, but his tone remained civil.

"I don't know why Marilyn doesn't move in with us. We've tried and tried to get her to."

"Gertie, I'll get coffee for everyone," Marilyn said quickly.

As soon as dinner was over, they moved away from the table. Gertie said, "Come into the den, Mr. Rankin, and I'll show you Jack's football trophies and his picture."

"Gertie," Marilyn said gently, "why don't we just sit down in the living room and talk."

Gertie's face flushed. "Oh, I'm sorry. You don't want to see Jack's trophies?"

Colly smiled tightly. "I'd be happy to, Mrs. Pearson."

For another hour they looked at trophies and old photo albums, and listened to Gertie and Ralph talk about Jack and Marilyn. Colly smiled and nodded pleasantly, listening attentively, but a muscle kept twitching in his cheek and his blue eyes were glacial. Every effort Marilyn made to change the conversation was defeated by one of her in-laws. Finally Marilyn couldn't stand it another minute.

"Gertie, we have to go now. Colly needs to see his parents too."

"Don't rush off," Gertie said, but Colly was on his feet and Marilyn had gone to get their coats.

When the kitchen door closed behind them, they walked to the car in silence, the leaves on the driveway crackling beneath their feet. As they sat down in the car, darkness closed in around them. Marilyn shivered from the cold, and from nerves.

She put her hand on his arm. "Colly, they were terrible to you, but they're scared to death they'll lose me."

He stared straight ahead, his jaw squared. "Sure enough, Mit. And you've given them one hundred percent of your loyalty. That doesn't leave me with much, does it?"

The words were like a blow, and she sensed the depth of his hurt and anger. With anguish she watched him reach into his pocket, then plop a small pill in his mouth.

"Your stomach hurting?"

"A little." He turned to face her. "A millionaire by thirty, and you're working two damned jobs," he said bitterly.

"He had everything we owned mortgaged by the time he was thirty-five. He did again when he was thirty-eight. We were on a financial seesaw. They don't know anything about it. Please, give them another chance."

"Oh, sure. I can tell how much they'd like to see me. Or did I miss an album of his achievements?" He started the car, driving too fast all the way to her apartment.

Outside, he parked the car, leaving the motor and the heater running as he shifted to face her again.

"Are you going to wear my ring?"

"Yes. I have it on right now. Colly, if we get married, where will I live? And work?"

"I have an office in Denver," he said stiffly.

"I can't go so far away from them. What ties you to Denver? Can't you move?"

"Will you marry me, Mit?"

"And live in Denver?"

"They're smothering you. They're in fair health. They have each other. They've been selfish—"

"Colly, dammit, don't!"

"Don't bring up again how they've let you work at night?" He hit the steering wheel with his hand and stared out his window. "Any ten-year-old kid could figure out why you hold two jobs. She needled me and needled me all evening. They've all but built a shrine to him, and they want to make you a sacrifice on it!"

"That's the biggest bunch of nonsense! You're angry, Colly, and you're not thinking."

"Are you going to marry me?"

"And live in Denver?" she repeated, feeling anger and hurt and frustration mix in her heart. He was being stubborn, she told herself, so unrelenting in his judgment of them. Of course they had behaved abominably to him. . . .

"Yes, and live in Denver. I don't give a damn if you fly home to visit them every week of the year. I don't care how many times you call them."

"That's not the same."

"No, it's not. They can't smother you that way."

"They're not always like this. They're scared of you."

"Yeah, and I know why. You're a doormat for them."

"You're being mean, Colly!"

"How much are you willing to give on this?" he asked quietly. "In essence what you're saying is that you'll marry me and give me the bits and pieces of time and yourself that they don't take. And I'll tell you something—they intend to take and take."

"We're not getting anywhere." Removing the keys from the ignition, Marilyn opened the door and stepped out. He let her go. She unlocked the door to her apartment as he stood beside the car.

"I forgot. You don't have a car. I'll drive you home." She stared through the darkness at him, a tight pain constricting her chest.

"I'll walk, Marilyn." The words were snapped off, so final, so angry that she didn't want to argue. She went inside and locked her door, letting the tears come. She rubbed the diamond on her finger. It had gone so badly. Gertie and Ralph had been terrible.

She wanted to fling open the door and run after Colly, but they would still be at the same impasse.

A week later she hadn't heard from him. By that time, Marilyn had come to a decision. She wrote to him.

October 26

Dear Colly:

Here's your lovely ring back. I've insured it and am sending it under separate cover by express mail.

This is what I was afraid of that first afternoon. I think some deep, instinctive feeling told me that if I went out with you again, I would get hurt badly.

I'm torn between my love for you and my duty to the Pearsons. I do love them, and they can be nice.

I know you want all of me. So do they, and I can't abandon them completely no matter how badly they act. They're Jack's family, now they're my family. They're like children, so vulnerable and alone. I made a mistake (more than one) allowing them to become so dependent on me, and I'll have to change that—but it will have to be gradual. It would be cruel to move away abruptly.

You're strong and handsome and loving, Colly, and I wish things were different, but they're not.

I love you. And I always will.

Marilyn

In spite of the fact that wisdom told her there would be no more letters from Colly, she held her breath every day when she opened the mailbox. Marilyn quit the job at Jose's, feeling desolate on the empty nights she sat at home. She spent Thanksgiving with the Pearsons and longed for Colly, wondering if he were in town.

She missed him, loved him, dreamed about him, and cried over him.

After Thanksgiving, the headlines once again took up the case of the Sterling Bank failure. Marilyn read the articles repeatedly, certain that Colly was in town again. At night she watched the television news coverage of the trial, hoping for a glimpse of him. By Thursday, her day off, she could no longer stand knowing he was in town and not seeing him. Even if they didn't talk, she had to see him.

As she dressed carefully in a tailored navy sheath dress, she thought about Mr. Rankin, who had always been friendly and cheerful, who had built the treehouse for Colly and let them help, something her own father wouldn't have had the patience to do.

She had to park a block away from the Federal District Court. She pulled her black coat collar up when a chilly gust swept across the yellowing lawn. Bare branches of tall elms were starkly outlined against the sky and a crew of workmen were putting final touches on Christmas decorations.

The holidays. Marilyn's thoughts veered away from the prospect, and she prayed with all her heart that Colly's father would be found innocent of any wrongdoing.

A short flight of steps led to a high-ceilinged hallway with marble floors. Her nerves tingled with anticipation. With each step, an inner voice whispered, "Colly, Colly . . ."

Six

In the courtroom she sat at the back, barely aware of where she was going or what she was doing. At her first glimpse of Colly's thick head of hair and his unmistakable broad shoulders, her heart went into an erratic beating. Behind his father, Colly sat staring straight ahead, and she desperately wanted to walk down the aisle, sit beside him, and hold his hand. While she was watching him, he squared his shoulders, then turned his head a fraction.

She held her breath waiting, her hands clenched in her lap. Without seeming to see her, he faced the front again, and she slowly exhaled. With a shock, she saw that Mr. Rankin had changed drastically. His brown hair was graying, his broad shoulders were a little stooped, and he looked almost gaunt. Mrs. Rankin's brown hair, combed into soft waves, was also sprinkled with gray, she noticed.

When Judge Trent entered, everyone stood. Marilyn watched the proceedings, unaware of anything except the terrible, condemning statements against Mr. Rankin and the all-consuming ache she felt for Colly.

If he had ever needed a friend, she thought, he needed one now. She wished she had called the Rankin house before the trial began. Questions jangled her nerves even more. Was the trial making Colly's stomach react? Where was he living and working now? Had he managed to forget her? How could she live without him?

To her relief, Mr. Rankin's lawyer presented a strong defense, but the charges and accusations were grim. The trial was a dreadful experience, she thought, and she hated that the Rankins had to go through it.

Finally it was over for the day. The spectators filed out until the only people left in the courtroom were Colly, his parents, two attorneys, and Marilyn.

Colly was talking quietly to them. She heard a low murmur of voices as they conversed. He stood, holding his mother's arm, discussing something with the lawyers.

Marilyn waited for what seemed an eternity until they all turned to go. At last, she looked straight into dark blue eyes, and her heart stopped. She wanted to run and throw herself into his arms, to hold him and tell him not to worry. His brow was creased in a deep frown and lines bracketed his mouth, lines that hadn't been evident to her before.

With an effort she remained where she was. They came down the aisle, the attorneys first, then the Rankins, and Colly last. As she waited, each step that drew Colly nearer made it more difficult for her to keep from rushing to him.

As they drew closer, Marilyn was shocked at the change in his mother as well as his father. Mrs. Rankin's forehead was lined with wrinkles and she was a great deal thinner.

The two attorneys passed Marilyn with brief, curious glances, and, as Mr. and Mrs. Rankin drew abreast, Mrs. Rankin spotted Marilyn. For a moment they just looked at each other. Then Marilyn put her arms around Mrs. Rankin and hugged her.

"Marilyn, it's good to see you again. So nice of you to come."

Marilyn felt a lump in her throat and a sting behind her eyes, but she smiled. "I'm sorry you all have to go through this," she whispered.

Mr. Rankin stood between Marilyn and Colly. During the time she was talking to his mother, then turning to squeeze his father's cold, dry hand with concern, she was constantly aware of Colly standing only inches away.

"Nice of you to come," Mr. Rankin said, but he gazed beyond her as if lost in thought.

Marilyn couldn't stand it another second. She reached around Mr. Rankin to take Colly's hand and give it a loving squeeze. Her fingers wrapped around his, and she felt suddenly as if she'd been drowning and had caught a lifeline. "It's good to see you."

He stepped to one side of his father where he could see her, but his blue eyes were unreadable. "Thanks for coming."

There was an awkward moment. Then, impulsively, Marilyn asked, "Would . . . would you folks like to come over for dinner?" She held her breath, wondering what had possessed her. She didn't have any-

thing planned, or enough food at home to feed four
people.

Colly's dark brows narrowed as he looked at her
intently. Mrs. Rankin took her hand.

"You're sweet as ever, Marilyn. Come home with
us."

"Oh, thank you, no. I didn't mean to intrude. I—"

"Nonsense. We have more food than we can eat.
Our friends have been grand. Now, you come right
along."

For two heartbeats of time she stood in indecision,
waiting to hear Colly add his invitation to his
mother's. When he didn't say a word, she knew she
should decline, but before she did, she was compelled
to look at him.

One more glance at his hard, set features and she
heard her answer as if it were coming from far away,
from someone else.

"Thank you, if you're sure—"

"Of course I'm sure."

With impersonal sureness Colly's hands closed on
her upper arms. Moving her aside, he stepped past
his parents, saying, "Just a minute. I want to speak
to the attorneys. You all wait in the hall."

Marilyn's skin tingled from his fleeting touch.
She'd caught a whiff of the unforgettable fresh scent
of him, and intense longing infected every fiber of her
being.

Colly walked out briskly. His dark suit fit him
flawlessly, she noted, setting off his bronzed skin.
Marilyn ached to hold him, to try and ease some of the
strain he was going through. When he joined them
outside, she began to take her car keys out of her
purse. Colly's hand closed on her arm.

"Ride with us. I'll bring you back for your car."

His eyes were impassive, his voice tight and controlled. She nodded, and when they reached the car, Mrs. Rankin insisted that Marilyn ride in front beside Colly. Marilyn sat with her back to the door so that she could talk to the Rankins.

"Last summer Colly and I went to look at the houses on Acorn. The nicest people live in your house now," she told them.

Mr. Rankin continued to stare vacantly ahead, but Mrs. Rankin smiled. "Those were wonderful days."

Colly watched the road, remaining quiet while the two women talked. The hurt Marilyn felt for him was mushrooming as the moments passed. It was unlike him to sit in grim silence, she thought. She had never seen him so tense.

"Our old house is for sale. It was empty."

"I heard that. Nearly everyone has moved away. The Bateses live in Arizona now. Ed retired."

While Mrs. Rankin went on talking, Marilyn reached over and took Colly's right hand from the steering wheel, locking her fingers tightly through his. His chest expanded swiftly, his fingers curling around hers in a fast, firm grip as he shot her a questioning glance.

She smiled at him and received a squeeze from his fingers in response.

As they rode the last block, past lawns lined with tall oak trees, Mrs. Rankin said, "Will you look at that! Everyone's here again."

Cars were parked on both sides of the street in front of the single-story red-brick house. Colly parked at the end of the driveway, and they all headed into the kitchen.

Three women stood up from the round oak table to greet them. "Oh, you're back. The key was under the mat, so we thought we'd come over and get a little buffet ready."

"How nice of you. Marilyn, come meet these people."

She was introduced to the ladies, then to their other friends who were sitting in the living room and family room. A fire roared in the fireplace and the house was filled with cheerful conversation. Within minutes Mr. Rankin was seated on a brown leather sofa in the family room, surrounded by friends who were talking about hunting. Colly stood with a group of people in one corner of the room, and Marilyn joined the ladies in setting out the meal. The round fruitwood dining table held platters of food—steaming slices of baked ham, thick loaves of homemade bread, a bowl of homemade coleslaw, and trays of dark chocolate and white angel food cakes.

Later, after dinner and the dishes were done, Marilyn sat on the stone hearth, warming herself by the fire. She looked at the Rankins and their friends, and couldn't help contrasting them with the Pearsons.

The Pearsons had made Jack their world; everything centered around him. Now, in a similar way, they had done the same to her, and she had let them. How different were Colly's parents with their large circle of friends.

Her eyes were drawn to him across the room. Colly had shed his coat. He stood talking to two men, one hand splayed on his hip, his shirt sleeves turned up and his collar open at the throat. Just to look at him made her tremble with yearning. They hadn't had a chance to say a dozen words to each other, but she knew where he was every second. And in spite of his easy conversation, she could see the tense set of his shoulders, the muscle that worked in his jaw, and his quick, worried glances at his dad.

Finally the fire died to glowing embers and the only guests left were their neighbors the Emersons and Marilyn.

"I'd better be getting home," Marilyn said.

Instantly Colly was on his feet. "Your things are in here."

As they left the room, he took her arm and they walked side by side down the hall. Inside a bedroom lit by a small dresser lamp, an open suitcase rested on the bed. Next to it, Colly's jeans had been flung in a heap on the blue bedspread. She entered the room ahead of Colly, then heard the door close. She turned and reached for him at the same time his arms went around her, crushing the breath from her lungs.

"Lordy, I'm glad you came today. Thank you, Mit."

She heard the hoarseness in his voice and fought back the burning tears that threatened. She had to keep from crying, she told herself, but it took every ounce of will she had.

"This is the hardest thing in my life." He ground out the words but they were muffled against her neck. "It's killing Dad. Every second, every hour takes a toll. I can't do anything about it except sit there and watch."

"I hate this for all of you." Marilyn tightened her arms around him. "His attorneys did a good job, Colly."

He released her slightly, his big body shuddering as he brushed his hand across his eyes. "I tried to listen to the case and imagine how it might sound to a stranger, but I can't do it. The prosecution has flung so many damnable accusations at Dad." Colly looked at her, his blue eyes like chips of ice. "You see how Dad looks. And Mom—she holds up for his sake all day. Then when he goes to bed, she falls apart."

"Oh, Colly!" Marilyn felt his pain, knowing Colly had to be the strong one for both his parents.

"That first day in the courtroom Dad flinched at every charge that was read." Colly frowned. "Mit, he flinched just as if someone were hitting him! He's turned into an old man in these past few months."

Marilyn let him keep talking without her saying a word.

"I sit there and listen, and there's not a damn thing I can do. I've never felt so helpless, so frustrated in my life. If they find him guilty, I don't think he'll survive."

She hugged him tightly to her. "Don't conjure up the worst, please, because it may not happen! Promise me, Colly. You won't think about it beyond what's happening at this moment. Promise me!"

She felt his chest fill with a deep breath. "I promise to try, but the thought hovers over me like some damned black cloud."

"Please try!" she begged.

"Their friends have been a godsend. Every night the house has been full of people. If the three of us had to sit here alone together, I think I'd have collapsed."

"No, you wouldn't have, because you're strong." She slid her hands up and down his back, then stepped back a fraction to look up at him. "Are you getting any sleep?"

"I'm all right," he muttered, running his fingers through his hair.

"How's your stomach?"

"Like a chunk of concrete. I saw the doctor this morning and got a prescription."

She stood quietly, looking at him and hurting beyond belief. He was the dearest soul on earth to her, she thought, and she couldn't do anything to make it better. "I wish to heaven I could help!"

He looked at her, then closed his eyes and crushed her to him again. "You've helped me just by coming today. Oh, Lord, it's good to have you here. It's a relief to tell someone."

They stood quietly for a long time, until there was a soft rap at the closed door. Through the door came his mother's voice speaking in hushed tones.

"Colly, the Emersons have left. Dad and I are going to bed."

Colly moved to open the door. "I was talking to Marilyn."

"I didn't want to interrupt, but just to say how nice it is to have you here with us, Marilyn."

Marilyn hugged Mrs. Rankin, noticing a faint scent of lilacs. "It's like being home to be here. You were always my second mother."

Mrs. Rankin smiled, looking at Colly for a second before she walked down the hall.

"Colly, I should go home," Marilyn said.

He held her coat, lifting her hair and barely brushing her nape, but each touch was special.

He slipped on a navy parka and they left together. In the car he pulled her close, their breath forming clouds that mingled in the chill air.

"It did mean a lot to her to have you there. I got a prescription for them today and I hope it helps them sleep. Dad planned on retiring in two years. Two years, Mit."

She listened while he talked on and on, until at last they reached the darkened courthouse.

"I'll follow you home and see you inside."

"I'm a big girl now. You don't need to, Colly. You go home—"

"Shh. You're wasting your breath."

She drove home, his car behind hers. At her door, he turned the key, then stepped inside to pull her to him again for a fierce hug. His voice was a rumble that wrapped around her heart as tightly as his arms held her.

"Mit, you're my best friend in the whole world. I've talked for the past hour, and you haven't said a word. I haven't asked how you are, if you're happy—"

"Shh, Colly. There's time for those questions later."

"Oh, Lordy, Mit . . ." He gave her another bone-crushing hug and she clung to him with all the strength she had.

"Do you work tomorrow?" he murmured against her hair, his breath warm across her ear.

"No," she heard herself saying. "I'll be there." *If I have to quit my job to come*, she added silently.

"I'll pick you up and you can go with me. I'll come over about midmorning. Their friends will be at the house for lunch and you can join us."

"Fine, Colly." Reluctantly she stepped away when he released his hold. She locked the door behind him, listening to his car drive away.

As she changed for bed, she was lost in thought, and it took her some time to fall asleep. The first thing the next morning she sat down by the kitchen phone, calling Gertie to tell her she needed to see her right away.

Seven

Dressed in a charcoal gray pin-striped suit and looking incredibly handsome, Colly picked her up shortly
before eleven and they drove to the Rankins' for
lunch. Marilyn, in a red wool dress with her hair in a
soft chignon, had deliberately chosen to wear something bright, trying to do what she could to add a
note of cheer. Again the Rankins' friends were on
hand, and the tension eased slightly until it was time
to go to the courthouse.

Every moment during the trial was agony for her.
The argument by the defense attorneys gave her some
hope. To her, it sounded convincing enough to acquit
Mr. Rankin. But the closing argument for the prosecution was damning, and she locked her fingers
around Colly's hand.

After hearing instructions from the judge, the jury
retired to make its decision. The time seemed to drag
interminably until the word came at last that the jury
was ready with its verdict. Marilyn clutched Colly's

hand tightly in hers, holding her breath as the bailiff handed the decision to the judge.

The judge read inpassively: "We find the defendant not guilty. The case is closed."

Colly crushed Marilyn's fingers. Court was adjourned, and Colly hugged her jubilantly. "Thank heavens! It's over, Mit! It's finally over and everything's all right!"

"Bill!" Mrs. Rankin's voice sounded stricken. "Colin!"

Mr. Rankin clutched his chest and slumped, falling out of his chair. An attorney caught him. As Colly vaulted over the railing, someone called for a doctor. The clerk said he would call an ambulance.

The brief burst of triumph swiftly became chaos. Marilyn hurried over to Mrs. Rankin as the men worked on Colly's father. In a short time the paramedics arrived to take him to the hospital. There was a flurry of activity and Colly came and spoke to Marilyn. "Mom will go in the ambulance and I'll take you with me."

"Give me your keys," she said. "I'll drive your car. You stay with your mother and dad."

He dropped the keys into her hand and Marilyn left, knowing the ambulance would get to the hospital long before she could. She took the freeway, driving with care, praying that Mr. Rankin would be all right.

She joined Colly and Mrs. Rankin in the emergency room waiting area where they sat in a tense silence until a physician appeared in the doorway. Colly crossed the room swiftly to talk to him, and she could see the relief on his face as they conferred. When he motioned to them to join him, Marilyn waited, letting Mrs. Rankin and Colly talk to the doctor alone. Colly glanced at her, then waved impatiently for her to join them, a big grin wreathing his features.

He pulled her to his side. "Dad's all right. He collapsed from exhaustion and stress."

Marilyn couldn't help smiling as the doctor told Colly and Mrs. Rankin that they'd keep Mr. Rankin overnight for observation, and that he was sedated and sleeping now.

Interrupting their conversation, a feminine voice came over the intercom: "Paging Mr. Colin Rankin. Mr. Colin Rankin. You have an emergency call at the desk."

Colly's jaw dropped and he swore. "What the hell's happened now?"

"Go see. Everything else has turned out all right today," Marilyn reminded him.

"Well, I know all my loved ones are safe, so I can take this with a smile. Come with me, Mit. Mom, we'll be right back."

His words were a shower of roses tumbling around her, Marilyn thought joyously. Although she tried to convince herself that he was talking only about his parents, her heart wouldn't listen. As they walked down the hall Colly squeezed her waist jubilantly.

"We won! And Dad's all right!" His voice changed, the tenderness in it unmistakable. "And you're here at my side." Abruptly he stopped, spun her around into his arms, and leaned down to kiss her, deeply, passionately, and long enough almost to cut off her breathing.

Stunned and on fire, she swayed as he released her when they heard the voice page him again.

"Mr. Colin Rankin. You have an emergency call."

Colly swore mightily, but then he grinned at her

and hurried to the desk. She waited a few feet away, the receptionist observing them curiously. Colly's grin never faded. He cursed again, but his eyes never lost their happy glow. He kept looking down at his watch, talking too softly for her to hear more than snatches of the conversation.

Then he hung up the phone, flashed his most charming smile at the receptionist, and asked if he could make a call. She looked as if she would gladly turn the entire office over to him, Marilyn decided.

Colly called the airlines and speedily booked a flight. When Marilyn heard the conversation she glanced at the wall clock. He had exactly thirty minutes to drive to the airport, buy a ticket, and catch a plane.

"Mit—"

"Is it a big disaster?"

"No, thank goodness, because no one was hurt. A wall fell in and smashed a little café. The owner is mad as hell and I have to run. I can't take you or Mom home. I'll call a cab."

"Take the car, Colly, you'll lose time waiting for a cab. We'll get the taxi. Then tomorrow we'll pick up the car."

"You're sure?"

"Don't argue, you'll be late. Colly, I wanted to—"

"I know, so did I. I'll fly back the instant I can. Oh, love—" He pulled her to him for another devastating kiss.

Then suddenly he was gone, dashing out the door of the hospital. He turned at the door to call, "Tell Mom good-bye. I love you, Mit."

She smiled and blushed, glancing at the reception

ist, who was staring at Colly. As the door swung shut behind him the receptionist looked at her.

"My goodness!"

Marilyn grinned. "I think so too."

It was another hour before she finally got home. She flung off her coat and shoes and sat down to write a letter.

November 30

Colly:

I wanted to talk to you and we never got a chance. I hope you don't have too big a disaster. Your mother told me you're working in Chicago now and she gave me your phone number, but at this moment you're up in a plane, so I'm writing, to feel as if I'm still in touch with you.

I had a talk with Gertie. Will you please give them another chance? Can we have dinner together? I'll cook this time. Please, Colly. I told Gertie that I love you, that I'm going to marry you.

Try, just one more time. They *can* be nice people.

I hate it that you have to rush off to Chicago and more trouble when I know you're exhausted. Worry, worry. I hope you get home soon. Let me know if you'll come to dinner. If you do, I promise to cook your favorite, pork chops and sauerkraut (now you know the depth of my feelings). I'm sure that, at five years of age, you were the only kid in the whole U.S.A. who loved sauerkraut (yech!). We'll have everything you like: black-eyed peas, corn bread, and (second only to sauerkraut in popularity), your favorite dessert, banana-butterscotch pudding.

Your mother said those are still your favorites. Weird, but typical.

I'll wear my best dress, my Captain Flakey ring, and my beautiful diamond necklace if you'll come.

Fatigue is finally catching up with me. I didn't get much sleep last night for worrying about my best friend.

Night, Colly. Wish you were here.

Mit

Marilyn mailed the letter the next day on the way to the Rankins' house. She drove Mrs. Rankin and a friend to the airport to get Colly's car, then went to work.

That night she and a friend went to a concert downtown, and she didn't get home until late.

The next day after work she had dinner with the Pearsons, staying until after ten o'clock. When she got home from work the following evening, there was a letter in her mailbox.

December 3

Dear Very Best Friend:

Your letter arrived. You're not working a second job again, are you? I called and called and called. Each day I think I'll be through here and can come home, but it hasn't worked out that way. It's a helluva mess, but right now the only thing that really gets me down is being away from you.

I'll go to dinner with the Pearsons under one

condition. In spite of your glorious offer of pork chops, sauerkraut, and pudding, I want to take everyone out to eat. You can cook all the yummy stuff for me alone sometime soon.

I never have understood why classy restaurants don't serve such a delicacy as banana-butterscotch pudding.

Mom told me you came by. Thanks. Dad's better. How'd he look to you? Mom sounded chipper as a robin.

I have something better for you to wear than the Captain Flakey ring. Of course, you could wear them both and impress people.

What do you mean by that remark "weird, but typical"? Am I typically weird?

I'm rambling because I don't want to end this. I'm counting the seconds, minutes, and hours until I get home. It better not be days.

We're going to work something out, my dear Mit. I don't know what or how, but I can't get along without my best friend. I'm only half here.

I paused for your laughter. I'll close now and mail this because I have to go talk to a man about a lawsuit. I'm ready to go stand under the pear tree again and watch the birds fly by. Or better yet, I'm ready to . . .

If I had written what was on my mind, the paper would have gone up in flames. Use your imagination. It involves you and me. And no one else.

Now I will tell you something, but when I see you, you are not to mention it. Not one word. Get all your laughing done before we're face to face, because 1) it was another near-disaster; 2) it's your fault. You have me in such a state of craziness, best friend. The first two days I was back at work, I rushed my tail off to get things done so I could fly home to Oklahoma.

I had two letters to mail and my payroll checks. The payroll checks were in a big manila envelope. Because I was thinking about big green eyes, the sexiest legs in the U.S.A., and the most luscious body—I flung everything into the mailbox— manila envelope, payroll, letters, and all.

Get your laughing done now, Mit. Don't bring this up again. It was after closing hours. I had to call the postmaster himself. The next pickup was at five A.M. I didn't want to miss them, so I had to drive over to the post office at four-thirty and sit outside in a snowstorm, waiting for the truck. See what you're doing to me! Talk about lobbing mudballs!

Let me know when you want to go to dinner. I'll let you know the first chance I can get home. Right now, I can't leave.

Hugs and kisses and mmmmmmm—a whole lot of mmmmmmm! Oh, my, I have to get home SOON. I love you, Mit.

Colly

The next day, Marilyn came home from work to find a large package left by the postman. She recognized the scrawling handwriting and raced inside, slamming the door on the cold, wintry day. She shook the package and studied the handwriting again, wondering what he had sent her. Then she snatched up a knife and cut the wrappings away, flinging them aside in her haste. She lifted the box top and pushed aside layers of tissue paper.

Staring up at her was Ezmerelda. The rag doll's dress was freshly laundered and starched, but it was the same old dress. While her face had a faint smudge on the cheek, her black button eyes, stitched smiling mouth, rosy nose and cheeks were the same. And she had the same curly yellow hair, the locks uneven from long-ago haircuts. She held a folded note between her stuffed hands. Marilyn picked it up and read.

Dear Mit:
Here's your old dolly back with BOTH ARMS. Much ado about nothing, huh? You always did stir up a tempest over the tiniest things. And it took two to pull off the arm, you know. If you hadn't stubbornly held on, I wouldn't have pulled off Ezzie's arm.

I thought you might want her. Save her, Mit, for our little girl. I love you.

Now I have redeemed myself, I hope, and never again will be known as . . .
Rotten Rankin

Marilyn's pulse drummed and she was filled with longing for Colly. ". . . *our little girl,*" she read again softly, feeling a blow as if someone had punched away all her breath.

She reached down to pick up Ezmerelda, and for the first time saw what had been hidden beneath Colly's note. Around Ezmerelda's neck was a blue ribbon holding Colly's diamond ring.

"Oh, Colly!" Marilyn said aloud, too happy to care that she was talking to an empty room. "Ezmerelda," she whispered with joy, but it was the ring she was staring at. She untied it quickly and slipped it onto her finger, closing her eyes in happiness. Whatever happened between them, she promised herself, that ring had to stay on her finger. She wasn't coming that close to losing Colly again.

She picked up the phone to call him, spending the next hour in futile efforts to reach him. Finally she took pen and paper in hand and wrote.

December 6

Dear Adorable Colly:

I am admiring my ring, holding Ezmerelda, and trying to call you. Where are you? I've called and called and called.

Oh, Colly, thank you. I can't wait until you're here. My ring is beautiful. It's staying on my finger this time.

Ezmerelda looks wonderful. Her hair is just like it was. She still has that bald spot in back where you were going to show me the proper way to cut doll hair. (I think you were being thoroughly Rotten Rankin then, although you acted terribly innocent.)

Her arms look fine. You're forgiven. You're more than forgiven. When you get here, I'll properly reward you. (Though proper isn't the right word for what I have in mind.)

How did you find her? That's why you were so curious about Lurlene! I should have known you had something devious in mind. That's the most interest you've shown in Lurlene in your whole life.

I'm glad she got over her crush on you and

found someone else because, Mister Adorable Rankin, you are MINE. (I hope.)

Colly, surely we can work things out. Let's try. You put Ezzie together for me and made her whole. Now try me. I only have half a heart. But it's all yours.

I love you. Love and kisses and mmmmmmm back to you. Mmmmmmmmmmmmmmm.

Mit

P.S. Your dad looks better. I stopped by their house yesterday. They're wonderful to me. How lucky you are to have them. Watch out for bricks. *Please* watch out for bricks. I need you.

She continued to call until one in the morning and fell asleep with the phone on the bed beside her pillow.

The next morning she stopped by the Rankins and learned that Colly was in New Jersey, that he had told his mom to give Marilyn the message, and that he said he would write.

His letter came the following day.

December 8

Dear Mit:

I can't believe what's happening here. I can't get away. I tried to call you. Our schedules don't fit together. We'll have to agree on a phone time— three A.M., maybe? Anyway, I called the folks and told Mom to give you the message that I got a call on another job and had to rush to New Jersey. It was a big one and I couldn't ignore it because I'm going to need a bundle to spend on this gorgeous doll for her honeymoon. Don't start sputtering. I got your letter and we will work things out. Indeed, we will. And if you get muzzy about it, I will get rotten. Thoroughly rotten.

You have half a heart! Miss Muzzy, I don't have anything but a big empty space that aches.

I can't tell you the date I can get free. I think there's a conspiracy against me, little demons determined to keep us apart. While I was in New Jersey, someone set fire to the building I'm to demolish here in Chicago. I know, you're thinking it would save me a job, but concrete and steel don't burn, only the wood. It just caused delays and complications. Four days from now the building comes down. I have to be here for the demolition. Want to fly up and watch?

I have to hear your voice. You should get this letter in three days at the latest. I will call that night, the eleventh of December at midnight.

Please stay home. I need to hear that sexy, sultry voice for just a few minutes. Do you have the foggiest idea what your voice does to me? Plenty, Miss Muzzy. You and Ezmerelda be good girls until I get there. Then Ezmerelda can be a good girl. I have other plans for you.

Mit, can you tell I miss you?

I love you.

Colly

The next afternoon Marilyn received another letter from Colly.

December 9

Dear Mit:

I figured I might as well write. We seem to be

jinxed on talking over the phone. But—I'm coming home! Make a dinner date with the Pearsons for Saturday night. I'll still try to call at midnight, but the way things are going, the phone lines in Oklahoma will blow away or mine won't work or you'll be out gallivanting around—or whatever you do.

I can't wait to see you. Put on your slinkiest dress and I'll buy you all the fried chicken you can eat. (Or steak or lobster or pork chops. You used to prefer chicken—has that changed?)

Think about honeymoons, Mit. Where would you like to go and what would you like to see?

(As for me, the above question can be answered in two words—*bed* and *you*.)

See you Saturday night, oh joy!

Night, sweet sexy Mit. I ache for you.

Love, kisses, hugs, and a bushel of nibbles in all the best places.

Colly

Marilyn dropped the letter, called the Pearsons, then tried to call Colly. Getting no answer, she pulled out a sheet of paper and wrote.

December 11

Dear Colly:

I tried to call, but you were probably out blowing up buildings. I don't think I'll ever be able to watch you work. We have a date Saturday night. And the Pearsons are coming. I'll keep my fingers crossed and look my slinkiest. Ha, ha. As if I could look slinky. You must have had some other lady in mind with that request.

I don't care where we eat or what we eat, because I probably won't be able to swallow a bite for looking at the gorgeous, sexy hunk who's my date. *My fiancé.* Oh, that has a nice ring. I'm engaged to Rotten Rankin! I'll be Mrs. Colin Corinthian Rankin. Does that mean I'll be Mrs. Rotten Rankin? You see, I'm counting on working everything out between us.

I miss you bushels and buckets. Hurry, hurry home. I showed Gertie and Ralph your ring, so they know we're engaged.

And, since you seem interested, I prefer seafood to fried chicken, but you can buy me anything you want, including pork chops and banana-butterscotch pudding. That's love.

Blow up everything and come home. I love you.
Me

P.S. You did one of your finest demo jobs on my heart, mister! It fell apart faster than concrete and steel from your dynamite. I can't wait for the midnight call.

At half-past midnight, Marilyn rushed inside the apartment, flinging down her purse and grabbing the receiver from the ringing phone.

"Hello," came over the line, deep and masculine. With his first word, a syrupy heat flowed in her veins.

"Colly, I was late getting home," she said breathlessly. "I had to cater a dinner in Edmond—"

"At midnight?"

"I had a flat tire and it took forever. I'm thirty minutes late and I was so afraid I'd miss getting to talk to you."

"I wish I'd been there to fix the tire for you. It's so damned good to hear your voice, Mit."

"The feeling's mutual. I wrote a letter and I hope you get it before you come home."

"We have a dinner date, then?"

"Do we ever! I'm going to hang on to you this time."

"That's the best news I've had in a while."

She glanced down at the phone, realizing he sounded worried. "Are you all right?"

"Yeah. It's just that this job is jinxed, but that's not what I want to talk about. I want to hear you talk, to listen to your sultry voice. Mit, you have the sexiest voice. . . ."

"My goodness, so do you!"

He chuckled, a deep, throaty sound that tickled her nerves. "I don't know about that. I just want to lie back in bed and listen to you talk." She had a sudden image of Colly's long, hard frame stretched out in bed, and her breathing grew shaky.

"Colly, what are you wearing?"

"Jeans and a blue sweater. Why?"

"I just wondered," she answered, picturing him more clearly and aching to be with him. "Thank you for Ezmerelda. What fun it was to get my ring back, and Ezmerelda back, and your card. Your very special card."

His voice changed to that husky tone it had in moments of passion or deep emotion as he said, "Mit, I've never asked you—do you want children?"

"Oh, Colly, of course I do! I want a blue-eyed, brown-haired little boy. Except I may not always be able to cope if he takes after his dad. I know how your mother got some of her gray hairs."

He chuckled. "You'll cope. And I wasn't that bad.

Now tell me everything you've been doing. Lordy, you're hard to get hold of over the phone. You talk, and I'll try to pretend you're here. . . ."

"Colly, I want to hear about you. I can hear myself talk anytime."

"Humor me, Mit."

He sounded so earnest, she decided he might really need to hear her. "Okay, but first I want to know when to meet your plane. What time do you arrive?"

"Thanks, I'll rent a car. I'll be by around seven. Now talk, Muzzy."

"Well, I saw your folks yesterday and your dad looks better every time I see him. Your mom baked an apple pie and, of course, I had to have a piece. She really can cook. You know, if we get married—"

"When, not if."

"When we get married, well, I'm not quite the cook your mother is." There was a moment of silence and she realized he was waiting for her to continue. "I saw Gertie and Ralph today. I took Gertie to the dentist, then to the grocery. I wrote to you that I showed them the ring—"

"Save any volatile subjects until I'm where I can get my hands on you," he said softly. "Go on. What else did you do today?"

"I saw the cutest lost dog. It didn't have a tag. I rang doorbells and tried to find the owner, but I couldn't, so I brought him home and I read the ads and sure enough, I found the owner. They had a little girl who was overjoyed to get him back and it made me feel so good. By that time it was almost four o'clock and I had a dinner to cater—Colly, this is dumb."

"It's heaven."

"You're crazy. And it's costing you a fortune."

"I can afford it. I haven't spent a dime on you in months."

"Before all the money runs out, I'd like to hear you talk. You know, I miss you too."

"Okay, Mit. I'll take a turn in a minute. Now, tell me about everything since I left you standing in the hospital lobby."

"In the hospital. Well, the receptionist was overcome by your sexy charisma. I thought we'd have to scrape her up off the floor, but since I was also overcome, I couldn't do anything to help the poor girl."

He chuckled softly. "I love it, Mit. Keep talking. Why didn't you tell me years ago that I had sexy charisma?"

"Years ago?"

"Go on and talk. What happened next?"

She told him, talking on and on. She kicked off her shoes and pulled the phone over to where she could stretch out on her blue velvet sofa. She curled up on her side and kept talking until finally she said, "Colly, you'll owe all the money for our honeymoon to the phone company. And besides, my life is boring."

"Not so. It's incredibly fascinating."

"You can't afford to keep talking to me. Hang up and I'll call you back. I'll pay while you talk to me."

"No way. Talk about a life that is unbelievably boring. Without you, my days are blah and more blah."

"I like to listen to you talk just as much as you enjoy hearing me, but now we can't afford it."

"Shut up already, Mit, and I'll talk. I can afford it. I miss you. I dream about you. I want to be with you. We'll work everything out. But we won't discuss it long distance. No personal problems on long-distance calls. Now, where are you and what are you doing?"

"I'm talking to you!"

"Standing in the kitchen?"

"No, I'm curled up on the sofa."

"Better," he murmured, his voice lowering. "I wish I were curled up with you so I could feel you against me, touch you, kiss you. . . ."

The temperature in her living room jumped to tropical levels and Marilyn couldn't breathe. She rolled over and closed her eyes and let his words work their seductive magic on her nerves.

"I want to touch you—there and there. . . ."

She groaned. "Colly, hurry home. You were supposed to talk to me, not make love to me over long distance."

"You don't like love over long distance?"

"It's frustrating."

He sighed. "That it is. Have you thought about a honeymoon?"

"Isn't that a little premature? We have a few differences to iron out."

"We'll iron them into nothing."

"This is costing you an enormous sum."

"So what? Don't spoil my fun."

She settled back again, and they talked for another hour until finally her voice became drowsy.

"Colly, I had a dinner for one hundred people tonight and I'm sorry, but I'm getting sleepy. I'd tell you to talk to me, but I might fall asleep and you'd have to pay a huge long-distance phone bill to hear me sleep."

"Go to sleep, Mit," he ordered in his husky voice fanning the flames of longing. "I wish I were there to hold you."

"Then I wouldn't sleep," she murmured. "I love you, Colly."

His voice was filled with amusement. "Hang up the phone, Mit. I don't want to pay for silence. Night, Muzzy," he said in his sexiest drawl, stirring her a fraction.

"Night, Colly," she drawled right back. She heard him groan before the phone clicked. She replaced the receiver and fell asleep on the sofa.

On her afternoon off she went shopping for a dress to wear Saturday, finally deciding on a simple black sheath that on a different body might have been termed slinky. She gazed at herself in the mirror. She was not the slinky type, she thought regretfully, but the dress molded her figure and had a deep slit in the skirt that didn't show until she walked. She bought high-heeled black patent sandals and a matching bag to complete the outfit.

Saturday night she was dressed and ready by six o'clock. She wore the diamond drop around her neck, its brilliance flashing against the black of her soft crepe dress. Her hair was turned slightly under in a pageboy, framing her face. She paced the floor, anxious to see Colly, still nervous that the Pearsons would treat him as they had before.

The chimes rang at a quarter to seven and she swung open the door, letting in a chilly blast of cold air that she didn't notice or feel.

Eight

Colly filled the doorway, his charcoal gray suit show-ing beneath an open gray topcoat. He caught her in his arms and crushed her to him, then held her away to look at her as he stepped inside and closed the door.

"Lord-a-mercy, Miss Muzzy," he said softly as his gaze lowered, lingering on her breasts and making her throb with desire. As she drew a deep breath, the peaks thrust against the soft crepe. He raised his brows and a smile played around the corners of his mouth, but his gaze continued a burning trail downward.

"That's slinky enough to make my blood boil," he told her in a raspy whisper. His gaze traveled up and he held out his arms. She flew into them instantly. The moment his mouth met hers in the first hungry kiss she felt longing burst into white-hot flames. She clung to him, kissing him passionately. Finally, she interrupted the kiss to pull away.

146

"Colly, we have to go. . . ."

"Mmmmm," he murmured against her throat. Then he straightened and exhaled. "Okay, but I hope it's a short dinner. I'm having a slinky bonbon for dessert."

She laughed. "I'm a slinky bonbon?"

He grinned and picked up her hand to look at his ring on her finger. Looking satisfied, he held her coat, wrapping his arm around her shoulders to pull her close beside him as they stepped into the cold darkness.

They picked up the Pearsons, who sat a bit uncomfortably in the back seat of the car. The silence was broken by Colly as he talked about the weather, then about the day's headlines. The Pearsons were quiet and reserved, and Marilyn felt as if she were holding her breath forever.

As they drove swiftly along Northwest Expressway, Gertie said, "I found some pictures I wanted to show you."

Marilyn's heart sank. "Gertie—"

"They're some of your baby pictures, Marilyn, and I think Mr. Rankin is in them. There's a thin boy hanging off a tree limb beside you."

Marilyn laughed and relaxed. "That's Colly, all right. How'd you find the pictures?"

"There was a great big box of them in the closet. You must have left them at our house a long time ago. I'll show them to you in the restaurant where there's light."

There was a moment of silence, then Gertie said, "We're so proud of Marilyn, Mr. Rankin. She caters dinners, you know."

"That's what she told me."

"The restaurant uses some of her recipes."

"No kidding!" Colly glanced at her and she smiled.

"I don't know how she does it. She's given dinners for over five hundred people."

"Has she really?" Colly smiled, impressed.

Marilyn pointed to the right. "That building is brand-new, Colly. And a new hotel is going up a block away from here. It's amazing how much the town has grown." She turned to the Pearsons. "Colly's working in Chicago now."

"Are you? It must be cold there."

"It was twenty-one degrees when I left today."

"I don't like the cold," Gertie said. "Marilyn's so wonderful to come and sweep off the driveway when it snows. I worry so if Ralph does it."

"Oh, Mother, I take my time," Mr. Pearson spoke up.

"If you've known Marilyn all these years, you must have seen her wonderful paintings, but we were just amazed at how talented she is."

"Gertie"—Marilyn ran her hand across her brow, suddenly understanding that Gertie deemed her a safe topic and was going to stay with it—"Colly doesn't—"

"Oh, yes, Colly does," he interrupted swiftly with laughter in his voice. "I'm learning all sorts of things about you. No, Mrs. Pearson, I didn't know Marilyn could paint at all."

"Oh, my goodness! She does fantastic watercolors. She even had her own show."

Colly glanced quickly at her, his brows arching. Marilyn shrugged, smiling a bit embarrassedly.

"We have one of her pictures over the mantel. She's a wonderful painter."

They parked the car outside the restaurant, which had an interior designed to resemble a ship. Relieved to get out of the car and away from the topic of herself, Marilyn led the way inside while Colly held the door for everyone. Subdued lighting shed a golden tint over the rough oak planks of the walls and floors, the oak tables and captain's chairs. As soon as they were seated, Gertie said, "This is a lovely place. You know, Marilyn planned the interior of her house and you couldn't tell it wasn't done by a professional decorator."

"That's right," Ralph seconded, and Marilyn wanted to throw up her hands in exasperation. It wasn't as bad as before, but it embarrassed her. She glanced at Colly, who grinned and leaned forward to speak. "I didn't know Marilyn was so talented. All I've seen her do is lob mudballs and hit a target at forty paces."

Gertie looked surprised. "Mudballs?"

"I used to throw mudballs at him, and vice versa," Marilyn said. "What's everyone going to order?" she added, changing the subject.

"I'll have the chicken-fried steak," Ralph decided quickly.

"That sounds good, Dad, so will I. Mr. Rankin, you must get Marilyn to make you one of her fabulous lemon pies. It melts in your mouth."

"Her chocolate cake is my favorite," Ralph said. "We were so lucky to get a daughter like Marilyn."

Marilyn patted her father-in-law's hand. "You both are sweet, but you're making me blush."

"I love it," Colly said, giving the Pearsons his undivided attention and his best smile. "She's my favorite subject, and I never knew about all her talents because she wouldn't mention them."

"Oh, Colly, come on! Are you going to watch the Dallas Cowboys game on television tomorrow, Ralph?"

"Sure thing."

"Don't change the subject, Marilyn," Gertie said, beginning to warm to Colly's smile. "Your young man wants to hear how smart you are, so we'll tell him."

"Oh, she's smart, all right," Ralph said as Marilyn shot Colly a murderous look.

His grin widened. "What else can she do?"

"She types," Ralph said.

"You should hear her with a typewriter," Gertie added. "Just makes the keys fly. I can't work one of the things. I never did know how to type, but Marilyn is a whiz."

To Marilyn's relief, a waiter came, and they ordered. But as soon as he left, Gertie commenced again. "You must see Marilyn's paintings soon. They are really beautiful."

"I'd like to see them," Colly said, looking at Marilyn with curiosity. "I didn't know you painted."

She shrugged. "I haven't had much time lately."

"Oh, the pictures!" Gertie fished in her purse and pulled out a stack of old photographs.

"The crowning touch," Marilyn said dryly, and Colly chuckled.

"See, here's one with a boy hanging out of a tree." Gertie peered at the picture, then at Colly. "Is that you, Mr. Rankin?"

"Call me Colin, please." He took the picture and Marilyn leaned close to him, catching a whiff of the special scent that was Colly. Her shoulder touched his as she looked at the picture of them together. She stood smiling in front of the pear tree, her front tooth missing. Colly hung by his knees, making a face at the camera.

"I don't know why you didn't recognize him," Marilyn said with great innocence. "He hasn't changed a bit."

The Pearsons laughed and Gertie handed her another picture. This time Marilyn was younger. She stood in a frilly dress, ready for Sunday school, while Colly, dressed in short pants, a white shirt, and a neat little bow tie, was holding her hand.

"Oh, for corn's sake," he muttered. "The way my mother used to dress me! We'll burn this one."

"No, we won't!" Marilyn snatched it away. "It shows your fascinating knobby knees."

Colly grinned and winked at her.

"Isn't this cute?" Gertie handed them a picture of Marilyn in first grade, her front teeth missing, her hair in a shaggy, uneven cut.

"This is the one we burn," she said darkly.

Colly held it at arm's length and smiled as he looked at it.

"What happened to your hair, Marilyn?" Ralph asked, peering at the picture through his spectacles.

"I tried to cut my own hair. Give me that, Colly Corinthian."

His smile grew. "I think it's adorable." He tucked it into his coat pocket.

"Now, this is precious," Gertie said, and handed them a picture. Colly looked about twelve and he stood with his arm around Marilyn. They were in Halloween costumes, Colly dressed in his dad's army fatigues, Marilyn as a cat with whiskers drawn on her face and a black cat costume.

"Remember, you used to take me with you for trick or treat," she said.

"Yeah. We'd go together until I thought I was too big for a tagalong like you. Then you and I went out early and I took you home, so I could go again later with my friends."

She looked up at him. "I remember the first year you wouldn't go with me. I was in fifth grade. That hurt."

They had moved close together to look at the pictures. In the dim light his lashes were dark shadows, his blue eyes clear, his mouth so perfect, slightly sensual. Marilyn forgot the restaurant, forgot the Pearsons, and just stared at Colly. She wanted to lean closer, to touch him. And she saw the desire flash in his eyes, a look of hunger so intense it startled her into an awareness of what they were doing. She straightened then, her cheeks growing hot.

Gertie was blinking rapidly, and Marilyn realized her mother-in-law was on the verge of tears. She squeezed Gertie's hand, feeling compassion, hating the idea that they would have to grow apart, but hopeful that Gertie would let her go willingly.

In spite of Marilyn's efforts to change the conversation, Gertie and Ralph talked about her straight through dinner. When they stepped outside, snowflakes were tumbling swiftly to earth, a blanket of white already covering the ground.

Stopping the car in the Pearsons' driveway, Colly left the motor running and climbed out to go to the door with Gertie and Ralph. He disappeared inside the house with them and the minutes passed. Suddenly Marilyn wondered what was going on. He'd been gone too long just to be telling them good night.

The car windows fogged over slightly as she stared at the swirling, feathery flakes. Only one subject held her attention. At that moment, she realized, their differences diminished to nothing. In the next few minutes Colly would come home with her. She quivered with longing, aching to be held in his arms, to kiss him, touch him, do all the things she had dreamed about since their argument. Finally she saw him standing in the bright yellow light of the open kitchen door. Snowflakes swirled down on his broad shoulders, sprinkling his dark hair with white as he talked to the Pearsons. Then their door closed and he walked to the car.

He slid inside, bringing a rush of cold air and wet snowflakes, and she was in his arms instantly.

"I can't wait any longer, Colly." He kissed her hungrily and she returned his embrace, weaving her fingers through his hair as icy drops of melting snowflakes soaked her hands.

Finally she wriggled away. "We'd better go."

"Okay, Mit," he drawled.

"What was that all about?"

"I thought I ought to talk to them a minute. Just a friendly conversation. I wanted to tell them that I love you and I'll be good to you and I won't take you completely away from them."

"I imagine Gertie cried."

"Don't you get worried. Not now. We'll talk about it later."

And she was willing to settle for later. She shifted in the seat and brushed her hand along his arm, irresistibly drawn to him. "They were better than last time, but that was the second most embarrassing evening I've ever spent."

He laughed, the deep-throated chuckle that always played havoc with her nerves.

"I had a very good time. My favorite subject—and my, oh, my, all the things I learned."

"Oh, Colly, don't be silly. They put Jack on a pedestal and he could do no wrong. Now they've done the same with me. My lemon pie is a lemon pie. My chocolate cake isn't as good as your mom's. I type at an adequate speed. I'm no paragon of—"

"Pshaw, ol' modest Muzzy. I want to see your paintings."

"They're not that special. And you can't because I sold them."

His head whipped around. "It's a wonder you didn't cut off your hair and sell it! You sold all of them?"

"Colly, don't start something."

He hunched his shoulders and rode in silence, but their problems had intruded and changed the mood. She smoothed her coat over her knees and watched it snow through the sweep of the windshield wipers. When they reached her apartment, it was impossible to park close to the door.

"I should have worn boots and a sweater instead of these slinky sandals."

"Just stay right there." He came around the car and scooped her into his arms to carry her inside. When he kicked the door closed behind them, he lowered her gently until she was standing. She trembled with her need for him, but she stepped away quickly. "We might as well talk it over, Colly, because we have to face the past before going on."

She hung up her coat and took his topcoat. "Would you like something to drink? Hot chocolate?"

"Sure, hot chocolate is fine."

As they entered her tiny kitchen, a chair scraped at the table. She got out a pan and the milk, then glanced at him. He was hanging his suit coat over the back of the chair. He loosened his tie while he watched her with a steady gaze that made her forget what she was doing.

When he unbuttoned the top two buttons of his shirt, her mouth went dry. "Colly, we should talk—"

"We'll talk." He came toward her and she could see the overpowering hunger in the depths of his eyes. Her heartbeat drowned out all other sound and she couldn't move.

"We'll talk, I promise, but there's something that's more important right now." He took the milk from her hand.

"Colly, if you touch me, we'll never be able to be logical and—"

"Logic is a cold companion," he said gruffly, and pulled her into his arms, leaning down to cover her mouth with his.

It was like the touch of a match to dry tinder, and she went up like old kindling. She burned with need that she had banked and held in check for too long. She trembled and clung to him, kissing him with loving abandon, forgetting all disagreements, aware only that he was the most precious soul on earth to her.

The slinky black dress fell at her ankles and he picked her up to carry her to the bedroom. His voice was husky in her ear as he showered her with quick kisses.

"I'm going to show you how much I missed you, how much I need you."

*　　*　　*

Two hours later, she lay in his arms, watching snowflakes tumble against the windowpanes. "Colly, we've skirted the issue in our letters, on the phone, and finally tonight. We have to talk. Or did you plan on dating the rest of our lives?"

He laughed softly. "Hell, no, we won't date the rest of December if I have my way. I'd get married tomorrow if you'd stop being so muzzy. And that reminds me. Just a minute."

He stepped out of bed and left the room, returning with his coat. Marilyn barely noticed what he was doing as she drew a deep breath at the sight of his virile body that held not an ounce of fat, but only hard, trim muscles.

"How do you stay tan in Chicago in the winter?"

He glanced down at his body as if he were looking at the furniture. "I'm outside constantly, and my tan's slow to fade. And I have a tough hide."

"Hmmm. Too tough to feel this?" Feeling a constant need to touch him, she brushed his hip with her fingers.

"I think I felt something. Try again."

Laughing softly, she sat up in bed and pulled the sheet to her chin, watching the corners of his mouth lift in amusement. As he sat down, he flipped the sheet casually across his lap. He dropped a packet in front of her. "I just got this."

Raising her eyebrows, she picked it up and pulled out a thick sheaf of papers. "What on earth, Colly?"

"Insurance. You're the beneficiary on my policies and I just took out a new policy, that one."

She laughed. "Colly, for heaven's sake! I didn't know you were so practical!" She glanced down at the amount and was shocked. "My word, Colly! This policy must cost you a fortune in payments."

He lay back on the pillow next to her. "I have a little money."

"Oh, my."

"What?"

"I know what you mean when you get very modest. My goodness, Colly, you're worth a fortune!"

"I can see I'll never be able to keep anything from you. You'll know all my secrets without lifting a finger."

"And vice versa. Is your business that good?"

"It's a dangerous business. That costs. It's tricky and complicated. That makes it cost more. Also, dear Mit, I've traveled constantly, no big loves in my life, so the money has gone into the bank and into investments and into property."

"My word! I've never thought of you that way."

"What way? You still see me as the kid on Acorn Avenue who earned a living mowing lawns and throwing papers."

"I'm glad it's been good for you."

"So am I, Mit. We're going to have fun," he said softly, and she felt a quick tingle of excitement. Colly could be the most fun person on earth, she thought.

"I want you taken care of, whatever happens. You're never going to sell your damned paintings or car or house again to survive."

"You're sweet and impossible at the same time."

He grinned. "And you're sexy and muzzy at the same time."

Remembering the problem confronting them, she said, "Now stop being rotten. It takes two to make things work. What are we going to do?"

"I hope we're going to get married and live happily ever after in Denver."

"Is there any reason you can't move your business here? I won't let them smother me."

"I can't move it here, because you will let them smother you."

She drew circles on his furred chest with her finger. "What did you say to them when you went inside after dinner?"

"We talked just a little more about you."

"Did you ask them to get out of my life?"

"Oh, Mit." His voice was tender as he sat up and put his arms on her shoulders. "Of course I didn't. I wouldn't do that."

His eyes were wide and blue, his lips so close she had to touch them with her finger. "What did you say?"

"I told them how much I loved you, that I want to share you with them, that you can come visit whenever you want, but that you're young, you're entitled to happiness and a family and a home."

"And what happened?"

"I imagine you know. Was it bad when you told Gertie that you and I were engaged?" he asked gently.

"Yes." She could barely answer, thinking back to the hour she had spent listening to Gertie cry and reassuring her that she wasn't leaving forever.

"Mit, I'm sorry you have to go through this, but you've let them make you their whole world. How often do they get out of the house? What friends do they have? They don't go to a church, they have no hobbies except puttering around the house, they've got no close friends. They live unto themselves and have made you the center of everything now that Jack's gone."

"That's what I told you, but I can't just jerk everything out from under them at once."

He stared off into space. "We're back at the same impasse. If this were the reverse, if you were gone and Jack had a chance at marriage and happiness, would you want him to give it up to stay with your folks?"

"No, I wouldn't. But logic doesn't change how I feel. I just can't abandon them."

"I would have to fall in love with a damned tenderhearted woman."

She smiled, then grew sober as she thought about their dilemma. "Colly, why not move your office? Your folks are here, it's home. I promise—"

His hand covered her mouth swiftly. "Gertie was on her best behavior tonight because she's so terrified of losing you. But if we lived here, and she called up and said she was sick, you'd run right over. If she needs to go to the doctor, she'll ask you to take her. Before you know it, Mit, you'll be in the same situation. You can't promise it'll be different, because nothing will really have changed."

Her throat felt tight. "So we're back at square one."

"No, we're not. You keep my ring, we'll stay engaged, and we'll work on this. Come with me for a week and get away from everything. Maybe it'll give you a new perspective."

"I might do that," she said cautiously, trying to find some ground where they could meet and agree. "But I'll have to give them plenty of notice."

"All right, give them notice."

The shrill jangle of the phone interrupted their conversation.

Nine

With a sinking feeling, Marilyn picked up the receiver to hear Gertie's voice. "Marilyn, can you come over now? Ralph's having chest pains. I've called an ambulance."

"How soon do you expect it to come?"

"Right away."

"You ride with him in the ambulance, and I'll meet you at St. Mary's." She hung up the phone and looked at Colly's impassive face. "It's Ralph. He's having chest pains."

"I'll take you." Colly grabbed his clothes, disappearing into the bathroom. She heard the shower, and in less than five minutes, he appeared dressed in his slacks. He pulled on his shirt, buttoning it swiftly while she headed for the bathroom.

"Colly, you don't have to go."

"Get dressed, Mit."

She showered quickly and dressed in jeans and a blue woolen sweater. Colly was ready when she emerged. Swiftly he glanced from her head to her toes and back.

"You look wonderful, Mit. C'mon, don't worry until you have to. That's what you told me to do about Dad."

"I'm so sorry this happened now."

He shrugged and pulled on his topcoat. "Where's your coat?"

On the way to the hospital they rode in silence. Marilyn was miserable. Colly was taking the incident remarkably well, she thought, but it didn't relieve the tension she felt. The incident made it all the more difficult to think about telling Gertie and Ralph that she might move to Denver. That she wouldn't be around for emergencies.

They reached the hospital at midnight, and it was three A.M. before they were back at Marilyn's. Ralph had needed oxygen and was resting comfortably. If all went well, they were told, he would be home in a day or two.

The next morning Marilyn and Colly went to church and Sunday dinner with the Rankins and didn't have a chance to talk before they drove to the airport. Marilyn took her car so Colly could leave his rented one. Finally, when they reached the waiting area for his plane, they stood in an isolated spot in the hall to talk.

"We didn't solve anything," she said softly.

"Look at the bright side." He smoothed the collar of her coat, running his fingers back and forth over her collarbone. "We had fun. I made a truce with the Pearsons. And we're engaged. We'll take it a step at a time, Mit."

"You were so great about everything. So nice, so

helpful, so polite. I think Gertie is beginning to succumb to your charm." While she talked, she studied him, trying to memorize each feature as he stood there in his thick-ribbed brown sweater and cords that looked so good on him. She noticed a soft curl that fell over his temple and reached up to push the lock into place.

"You keep that ring on your finger, Mit. I'll think of a plan." His jaw thrust out, his blue eyes developed a determined gleam, and suddenly she had to laugh.

"Where have I heard that before?"

His eyebrows raised, he looked at her questioningly. "Where have you?"

"I think right before you boosted me up to the porch roof so I could climb up to the chimney and get down your kite."

He grinned. "I learned a lesson then. Don't boost a big crybaby who's scared of any height over a foot off the ground. They could hear you bawling clear down at Poe Elementary. And did I ever get it at home!"

They both smiled and he winked at her. "I'll come up with something."

"Each time you say that I get a little more nervous. That's your 'I'm-going-to-get-my-way' tone of voice."

"I don't recall getting this much argument out of you when we were younger."

"I wasn't as bright then."

"Have you given two seconds' thought to living in Denver?" He asked it lightly, but his voice was earnest.

"Yes, and I can't imagine it. What would they do in a crisis like last night?"

"They'd manage, Mit. Neither one has a friend or a relative they could call?"

"Well, not close, really close friends. And Gertie has a sister, but they haven't spoken for a year."

"Gertie has a sister." He said it quietly, but she felt a sudden chill.

"They don't speak to each other," she explained again, as if he were hard of hearing.

He swore quietly and long and so vehemently, she glanced around to see if anyone could hear him.

"Colly, for heaven's sake!"

A deep voice announced the boarding time for Colly's plane.

"Gertie and her sister might get back on speaking terms if you were out of the picture," he muttered in a low voice.

"Are we going to part with you angry?" she asked.

"Hell, no. I'm in love." He grinned. "I'm happy as a clam. Keep my ring on your finger and I'll work on this. But you do something for me. Give me about an hour's worth of thinking about living with me in Denver. Okay?"

"Okay, Colly," she said, and slipped her arms around his waist. "What I want is for you to come home with me and not go flying off to a job that's dangerous every day of the year."

He smiled, wrapping his arms around her waist inside her full-length coat. His hands stroked her back and she yearned to bring him home with her. "Sometime come watch me work. It might not be half as bad as you think, Muzzy Mit."

"Will the passengers in rows one through twelve now board," the announcer said.

"Colly, that's you."

"I'll go in a second. First things first." His hands

drifted slowly, sensually over her buttocks and pulled her close.

"Colly!"

"No one can see what I'm doing. I have to have something to think about when I'm on the plane."

"Sometimes you're so hopeless! If we marry—"

"When, Muzzy, when!"

"When we marry, am I going to spend half my life telling you good-bye?"

He frowned. "I know, I hate it too. If I had known I was going to marry the sex kitten of Acorn Avenue, I would have learned a profession in college that would let me stay home nights with you."

She laughed. "That's another—Colly, watch your hands!" He grinned as she wriggled free. "That's another reason to live here. All the time you're away it won't matter what I'm doing for the Pearsons."

"We'll see, Mit." His jaw grew firm again.

"That means a flat, unyielding 'no.' "

"We're not parting on a grim note, kid. I'll be back next weekend. This time, dinner alone at your place."

"Yes, sir!"

He chuckled. "That's more like it. And in the meantime—"

"Colly, there's the last call. You'll miss—"

"Mit." He crushed her to him one last time, to kiss her passionately until she knew she'd be glad to see him miss his plane. Finally he released her. "Hey, wait!" he called to the attendant who was roping off the entryway to the plane. As Colly sprinted toward the door, he looked back over his shoulder. "Write me today, Mit, so I get it soon."

"Sure, Colly. You write me too. Let me know what you figure out."

The sun shone brightly on the snowy landscape. The runways were clear and gray. Marilyn stood at the window, watching Colly's plane lift off and disappear into a sky as blue as his eyes, and she felt a sense of loss and despair.

She missed him terribly, and in spite of his determination, she didn't see that they were any closer to a resolution of their problem. She went by the hospital to see Ralph and learned that he would be going home the next day. She took Gertie out to eat, then finally went home to her empty apartment. The bed was still rumpled from the morning, and she could see Colly everywhere she looked, remembering him holding her on his lap at breakfast, remembering his laughter, the moments of making love. She sat down to write.

Sunday night, December 16

Dear Colly:

I'm writing just as you asked, but all I feel is emptiness. I miss you. And we're really not a step closer to marriage. I tried to imagine living in Denver and I see myself torn between love and worry. I'll keep trying, but will you try seeing yourself living here?

You can do that much. Thank you for being on your best behavior all weekend. The Pearsons thawed a great deal. I don't have much to say except I love you, and I miss you terribly.

Love,
Mit

She mailed it and took up her life without Colly. Wednesday, she received a letter from him.

December 17

Dear Mit:

I had to write. I've been deep in thought all day. I've put it all down on paper. There are some facts we're sure about:

1) We're in love.

2) We can't get along without each other. We're together so far, aren't we?

3) You don't want to move to Denver because of the Pearsons.

4) I don't want to move to Oklahoma City because of the Pearsons.

I think there is a logical solution. I'll be home this weekend. I want you to spend the weekend with me, away from the Pearsons, the Rankins, and any outside interference, where we can TALK this over thoroughly. (Throw in a few kisses and mmmmmmmms.) Okay?

I'm through with this Chicago job on Friday. Whoopee! I'll have to come back for the lawsuit if it doesn't get settled first. I have a lawyer working on it, and for now it's his headache. I have too many other worries to get worked up over a lawsuit. (The insurance my company carries gave the guy a generous settlement that would buy him a bigger café, but he's suing for stress to his nerves because of the worry it caused him. He thinks he has stress!)

I'll fly in, pick you up, and we'll go off to be *by ourselves.* Humor me. I know it'll be only four days until Christmas, but you can do all you have to do before I get home. And I'll bring you back late Saturday if I have to. Just give me Friday night and all day Saturday. Pack your swimsuit. (Don't get excited, we're not going far, but the hotel or motel will have a pool—you did finally learn to swim, didn't you? All you used to do was flounder around and hate going in the deep end, but I figured anyone as multitalented in the lemon-pie, typing, and paint departments as you has to know how to swim.)

I'm glad I'm out of reach.

I'll buy you all the grilled swordfish you can eat. It seems to go to all the right places.

I'm incredibly lonesome for you this week. I didn't know I could miss anyone this badly. I have to see your big green eyes soon or I'll wilt and di grate into little broken pieces. So, dear Friend of the Zoo, spend the weekend with me and let's plan a marriage. Better yet, let's get married and plan later. Double-quadruple-dare you. Quintuple-dare you with peanut butter on it!

Mom keeps giving me the fish-eye and asking me when I'm going to make an honest woman of you. I keep telling her you won't make an honest man out of me. It's not Mr. Colin Rankin causing all this delay. Look at the fuss you raised over ol' Ezmerelda, and she is just fine and back in your clutches. Stop raising such a fuss over this. Just do it my way.

I paused for your laughter. I love you. Oh, my dear Mit, how I love you. I want a month's honeymoon in some warm, tropical place. (I hope you weren't thinking of Alaska. We never did talk about it when we were together.) Let me know the answers to all my questions. I kinda liked the phone call. It beats a letter all to pieces. This is the seventeenth of December. You'll get my letter (it's my lunch hour right now—I took a long one to write to you) by the twentieth. I'll call that night at midnight. I'll start at ten o'clock in case (miracle of miracles!) you're home doing nothing. I love to hear your sexy voice. It does more for me than this furnace. By the way, it's three below zero here today. I'm freezing in this drafty hole I rented temporarily for an office.

Mom called the Pearsons to ask them for Christmas dinner. I presume she has also called you by this time.

I hate to stop, but work waits. And I want to get this off to you, so I can call you. (I've never known anyone before where I had to make an appointment to talk to him/her on the phone!)

All my love . . . every single bit,

Colly

P.S. The holidays loom. I WANT TO SPEND THEM WITH YOU. We can do it several ways:

1) Get married and spend them together.

2) You come stay at the folks' and we'll spend them together.

I sense a dark foreboding that you have already planned something that is neither of the above. I will cross my fingers and hope. Love, love, love . . .

Marilyn lowered the letter and wondered where they would go, picturing one of the state lodges. It would be more like Colly just to take her to one of the elegant local hotels and not waste time driving for hours. Well, that would be all right with her too.

She studied his letter, his logical, orderly num-
bering of the facts. Suddenly there was an answer
that seemed so plain to her. They could compromise
by living somewhere that was close to Oklahoma City,
but in another town. And the only other large city in
Oklahoma was Tulsa.

Tulsa was a beautiful city with hills and trees. She
could get home in two hours' driving time, less if she
flew. She could imagine telling Gertie that they'd be
living in Tulsa. And Hicks had two outlets in Tulsa.
She might not even have to find a new job. Too eager
to sit still, Marilyn paced the floor while she mulled
the possibilities.

She wanted to run and call Colly, but it was after
one o'clock and he wouldn't be in. Tulsa. A burden
lifted off her shoulders. Then she began to worry that
Colly might not view Tulsa the same way she did. It
might be too close to the Pearsons to suit him.

Later that evening she talked for three hours to
Colly, but didn't tell him her solution yet because
they'd both agreed to save the important subjects
until they were together.

Friday night came and she dressed carefully in a
furry white sweater, designer jeans, and black boots.
Her black hair was combed loosely over her shoulders. Her heart skipped with eagerness and hope that
he would like the idea of living in Tulsa.

When she heard his car slow and stop in front, she
ran to the door. Desire and love for him burned like a
bright, hot flame as she watched Colly climb out of
the car and come up the walk in his long-legged
stride, his jeans molded to his strong legs.

Ignoring the cold, she flew to meet him. He caught
her, kissing her soundly.

"Hey, you'll get pneumonia," he said softly. Together they went inside where he held her at arm's length to look at her. "Mit, you look so damned good!" he said in his sexiest voice that felt like an invisible, erotic caress.

"So do you," she said, and her own voice thickened, lowering to a soft, throaty sound.

"Maybe we won't go any farther than your bedroom."

"I'm not arguing."

He chuckled and pulled her close, his breath fresh, his mouth tasting of mint. She closed her eyes while her heart thudded as loudly as his.

He spoke again. "I have an elegant room reserved. I'm taking you out tonight. I want to give you your Christmas present early."

She moaned a mild protest. "Colly, I've wanted you—"

"It won't take too long to get there, and we can talk."

"I have something to tell you. I thought of a solution." Suddenly she wondered if it was as good an idea as she had thought.

"I'll be damned. So have I."

"You have?"

"What's yours, Mit?"

"You tell me yours first." Her mind raced. If he had something he had planned on all week, he might reject her idea immediately. She became hesitant about telling him.

He raised his eyebrows. "Okay, but get your coat and purse and we can talk in the car."

"Where are we going?" She opened the hall closet and pulled out a black, knee-length woolen coat.

"To Tulsa."

She whirled around to stare at him and suddenly started laughing. "I should have known!"

His eyebrows inched higher. "What's so fun—well, I'll be damned." He grinned. "I hope to hell I don't ever have to keep secrets from you. When did you think of it?"

"When I got your letter."

"And it's all right with you?" She saw the concern in his eyes, the tense set to his shoulders, and she flung her arms around his neck.

"It's wonderful!"

"Come on, Mit, let's go. I have to show you something." He looked at his watch. "You know, it's only four o'clock."

"I know."

"Well, I thought—"

"Oh, boy, here it comes."

"You haven't heard my idea," he said in mock aggravation.

"I know that tone of voice. Oh, do I ever know that tone of voice, because I learned the hard way. That's the tone of voice you used when you told me how much fun it would be to paint our garage green. That's the tone of voice you used when you said Sinbad would look cute if we gave him a furcut. . . ."

Colly grinned. "Trust me, Muzzy."

"Are you going to be Rotten Rankin?"

"Of course not!" he said with great innocence.

"All right. What's your big idea?"

"We still have time to run down and get a marriage license."

"And get married tonight?"

"No." He put his hands on her shoulders. "My folks

will want to be there and so will the Pearsons. And I want you to have a wedding dress. We could get married Monday."

"On Christmas Eve?"

"I can't think of a better way to spend Christmas Eve," he said softly, kissing her temple, trailing kisses to her ear, igniting her desire.

"Colly, I can't think when you do that."

"You don't say. Marry me, Mit."

"What about the long honeymoon?"

"We'll go the day after Christmas."

She pulled away a fraction to glare at him. "You've thought all this out—why didn't you let me know sooner?"

"There are some things"—he leaned down to kiss her throat, then moved to the corner of her mouth— "that . . . I don't like to write or talk about . . . on the phone." He showered light kisses on her and whispered in her ear, "Marry me Monday, Mit."

"Okay."

"It'll be—" He straightened. "Okay? Just like that?"

She laughed softly. "Sure, just like that. I told you, sexy Colly, that you weren't getting away again," she said in her sultriest voice.

The laughter faded from his eyes and that intense look of need she had glimpsed twice before flashed briefly. Then he was crushing her in his arms while he kissed her until she lost all thought and care and logic.

Outside, the snow had melted and Oklahoma's fickle weather had warmed during the day to a pleasant sixty degrees, dropping again as night approached.

The stop for the wedding license made them arrive in Tulsa about nine o'clock that night. Colly drove straight to a newer residential area in the far southeast section of the city. They topped a rise, then turned onto a road driving between rows of dark oaks.

"I have a confession."

"Uh-oh."

"I came back from Chicago Tuesday night. I called you long distance from Tulsa, not Chicago."

"My, you're getting sneaky."

"It was for a good reason. I had to get your Christmas present."

"You brought me up here in the woods to give me a Christmas present? I thought maybe we were going to park and neck."

He chuckled and pulled her close. "Not a bad idea, but I have a warm hotel room waiting and 'neck' is an inadequate word for what I want to do."

"Amen."

He squeezed her, turned off the paved road to drive over rough ground. As the car bumped, she sat up. "Colly, what on earth?"

He cut the engine and stopped, moonlight bathing the landscape in patches between shadowy forms of tall trees. "Here, Mit. Merry Christmas," he said in his bass voice that was a gift of warmth all by itself. He placed a small wrapped package in her hands.

She opened it carefully, drawing out the suspense.

"Lord-a-mercy, we'll be here until dawn."

"I like to save the ribbons from your presents." She raised the lid. A small brass key nestled on white cotton.

"Just what I've always wanted! Maybe." She held it in her hand. "What is it?"

He chuckled and climbed out of the car, pulling her gently out after him. "It's the key to our house, Mit, and we're going to build it right here. I was going to let you help select the lot, but when I saw this place, I had to make an offer before someone else did." He slipped his hands inside her coat, opening his to pull her close, crushing her soft breasts against his chest.

"I wanted to surprise you, Mit. I finished the job in Chicago early this week. I thought about Tulsa last Sunday night, so when I was through I flew down here to look. The real estate agent showed me houses and lots Wednesday and Thursday morning, and then we found this one. This had to be ours. Come look at this."

Taking her hand, Colly led her up a gently sloping, tree-covered incline. Dried grass and leaves rustled beneath their feet. Moonlight bathed Colly's face briefly and Marilyn felt a surge of happiness. She hurried to keep up with his long steps until suddenly he stopped.

"Now, guess why this was meant to be ours."

She glanced around at an empty hillside covered only in winter's yellow grass, brown leaves and bare, brown trees. Then she saw why.

A few yards away, with gnarled branches stretching skyward, a broken branch hanging at an odd angle, its rough trunk dark against the landscape, stood a large pear tree.

"Oh, Colly, our pear tree!"

They walked closer until they stood beneath the branches, admiring it. "I figured we'd plant one, but then I saw this lot. It's in a good part of town, a big, deep lot—I bought the one next to it too—and we already have our pear tree."

His voice became husky and he slipped his arms around her waist again. "Mit, we're going to put a swing on the branches and a bench beneath it and we're going to come sit here every night, just sit out here and enjoy life."

She felt tears sting her eyes and she hugged him tightly. "I'm going to cry, I'm so happy."

He growled a throaty sound, shifting so he could cover her mouth with his. His kiss tasted of her own salty tears and his minty breath, and then she didn't notice either of those things anymore.

He moved a fraction to nibble her ear. "When spring comes and we have our fence built, I'm going to bring a blanket out here and make passionate love to you right on this spot."

She laughed as she showered kisses on his throat, standing on tiptoe to reach his lips again. "Whatever you say, Colly."

"Let's go find that warm motel room, woman. We've dillydallied too long. . . ."

Ten

Christmas Eve they were married, and two days later they left for a month's honeymoon on a tropical island where the sand was white, the water blue, and Marilyn barely noticed either for looking at Colly. They returned to Tulsa to live in a two-bedroom condominium until their house was built, and Colly went back to work.

June 3

Dear Colly:

It's heaven to be in our new home, but oh, do I miss you more than ever—or did I just tell you that when we talked on the phone? Work at Hicks keeps me busy during the day, and even though there are still things to do to finish decorating the house, the nights are agony. I didn't know I could miss someone this much. Would you rather I didn't tell you? I don't want to worry you.

I got the phone bill—also amazing—I didn't know phone bills could run that high. It might be cheaper if you'd fly home every night. Hurry home. And please *be careful*.

Love,
Mit

In three days she received a letter from Colly and sat down to read it.

June 3

Dear Mit:

This is for the birds. I can't stay away from you. It's worse now that we're married than it was before. Let's put our heads together (and a few other parts together) and come up with a solution. Crank up your muzzy brain and find a way to keep me home or—would you like to go into demolition? Would you like to be a traveling secretary for a man in demolition? I know what a whiz typist you are.

See you Friday night. We have a date with a bed. Just the three of us. My plane arrives at half-past five. Let's see if we can be in bed by six. We can eat dinner at midnight.

I love you . . . oh, dear Mit, how I love you!
Colly

She folded his letter and smiled, thankful he had asked her to try and think of a solution to their separations. She had thought of one long ago, but hadn't known when or how to bring up the subject. Friday, she dressed in new jeans and a pale yellow shirt, and drove to the airport to meet Colly's plane.

Two hours later, when she lay in his arms, she brought up the subject.

"I cranked up my brain, Colly."

"I hope it didn't hurt."

She chuckled and drew circles on his flat stomach, leaning over him while her black hair fanned across him, a dark tangle above the short curls that matted his chest. "You have lots of money."

"And you're going to spend it."

"Will you let me talk?"

"Sure enough. Can't stop you." He laughed and hugged her. "Go on. I'll be good."

"Impossible. All right, here goes. Get a business here at home."

"Sure. But you're the one with all the talent. All I know how to do is play football and tear down buildings. I'm too old and out of shape—"

"*Au contraire!* This body, out of shape?" She trailed her fingers along his thigh.

He groaned and caught her hand. "Now who's interrupting?"

"You don't like that?"

With a flash of white teeth he grinned. "Talk fast, and then I'll show you how much I like that."

"I've thought about our future." She looked at him seriously. "There's a business I know. We could go into it together. You know how to keep books, how to run a company. You would be the owner."

"And you would be the boss." He laughed softly. "I don't know an iota about catering or running a restaurant."

"With your brains, you'd catch on quickly. I wouldn't be the boss."

He hugged her to his chest. "It's okay with me if

you're the boss. Do you really think we could make it work, Mit?"

He sounded so earnest her heart skipped rapidly with hope. "It's a risk. If we fail, it'll cost you a lot of money."

"Cost *us*," he said softly. "It's us now, we and ours, Mit. Not yours and mine. How much money would it take the first year?"

"Just a minute." Snatching up her robe, she pulled it on and left the room. She returned with a tablet and sat down beside him on the bed. "What are you smiling about?"

"How long have you been thinking about this?"

"Mmmm, a while. I miss you terribly when you're gone."

He kissed her, then sat up beside her, the white sheet draped over his lap as he looked at her figures.

She leaned against his warm, bare chest and began, "It depends on how big and how fancy you want to go. We could start with something simple, a limited menu, yet enough variety that the food would appeal enough to people to want it catered for parties. Even then, it's an incredible amount of investment. And my figures don't include a building and lot—that's your field."

They sat and talked for another two hours, then moved to the kitchen to continue the discussion over dinner.

Saturday morning Colly asked a real estate agent to look for possible sites. Sunday they drove to Oklahoma City to visit the Pearsons and Rankins, and on Monday morning Colly left for his job in Cleveland.

That Wednesday, Marilyn received a letter.

June 10

Dear Mit:

You must be at your Friends of the Zoo meeting. I called and called. I'll call again and probably tell you everything that's in this letter, but I like this habit of writing you letters and I can't break it. It makes me feel a little closer to you.

You know, Mit, it's funny. I never wrote letters to my folks. In college, I think I wrote twice asking for money, and the year they sent me to summer camp when I was twelve, the camp director made us write our parents or we couldn't eat Sunday dinner. The letters have been fun, but it's a whole lot more fun to have you in the next room or the same bed or the same town. I've made some appointments to talk to a couple of men in Tulsa who have restaurants. I like your idea of a steak house. I don't want to take the time to build. You start planning a menu and the décor, and so on. Let's find something that's already standing that we can redo and get going quickly. I want to be home with you all the time.

I'll be through with this job by the end of June if all goes well. I planned the time off because I thought we'd take a vacation. Instead, we'll plan our restaurant. This is coming at a good time for me because I'm not booked into the months ahead. I can QUIT and COME HOME. Whoopee!

I'm so excited about this, Mit. I think it's the grandest idea. When we get the restaurant on its feet (or whatever thriving restaurants do) how about thinking about a family?

You know what Aunt Phoebe said. I don't want to get too feeble to be a father.

I love you. What an understatement. Dear Mrs. Big-Green-Eyes Rankin, how I love you. Plan fast, Mit. We're missing lots of good nights together.

Colly

Eleven

On a late fall afternoon Marilyn turned into the driveway, climbed out of the car, and hurried up the walk. Overhead the sky was a bright, clear blue with warm sunshine pouring over the front yard. A few oak leaves had turned yellow. Shifting the bag of groceries in her arms, Marilyn elbowed the front door closed.

"Colly! I'm home."

She looked through the mail and called again. "Colly!"

Silence was her only answer and she frowned, wondering why he wasn't home. She dropped her purse and carried the groceries to the kitchen. A note secured by a red tomato magnet fluttered on the refrigerator, and she pulled it down and read:

October 17

Dear Mit:

We're having an Indian summer day. The

weatherman just predicted it would be eighty degrees this afternoon.

There's logic—and then there's the heart. My heart is giving me different messages than my brain. The restaurant is off to a flying start due to your expertise. It looks grand, the books look super, the business is great.

What isn't great is that you work days and I work nights.

Now, you've trained a very capable manager. Let's *let him manage.* Let him take over nights, I'll take over days.

We took a risk in going into this business, and I LOVE IT! You'll never know how much I love it. I don't have to worry about bricks falling on innocent bystanders, or blowing out all the windows in the downtown area, or blowing up myself. What a marvelous idea you had.

Now I have a terrific idea. It's a beautiful day. If you'll step to the window, you'll see a blanket spread beneath the pear tree and a lazy fellow who's terribly in love with you stretched out on it.

Dear Mit, will you retire now and let us start that family? I've even thought of a possible name for our daughter—Mitzie.

Dear Mit, will you come out to the pear tree and play?

All my love,
Colly

Marilyn dropped the letter and went.

THE EDITOR'S CORNER

I have to be brief in this Editor's Corner because one of my designated pages is devoted to a short questionaire that I *do* hope you'll fill out and return to us. But, then, why do I need a lot of space when I simply can rattle off four names—Sandra Brown, Joan Elliott Pickart, Barbara Boswell, Nancy Holder? That's the quartet of wonderfully creative writers who are bringing you four marvelous LOVESWEPT romances next month.

Sandra Brown outdoes herself with **RILEY IN THE MORNING**, LOVESWEPT #115. That title has a special twist to it that I won't reveal. However, I can tell you that Jon Riley is the hero . . . and after an acquaintance of 182 pages with him, I cannot imagine any woman not singing *Riley All The Time*! You'll relish heroine Brin Cassidy's tumultuous twelve hours with her roguish ex-husband as they review their personal and professional months together. And when sunrise bathes these two heartwarmingly emotional characters in its golden glow, you'll rejoice at the ecstatic resolution they find for their problems. Hooray for Sandra Brown!

Petite Ashley Hunt storms into Ryder Cantrell's office just as she'll storm right into your heart in **MIDNIGHT RYDER**, LOVESWEPT #116 by Joan Elliott Pickart. Ashley's spunk coupled to her sweetness of character bring self-assured, impressively masculine Ryder right down to his knees. He's under contract to demolish the warehouse in which she conducts her plant business—and soon he believes she has him under contract to demolish his emotions! This is a tender, fun-filled, and exciting romance from Joan who is becoming so well known for her witty and wonderful and special romances.

Marvelously fresh and vibrantly original characterize all of Barbara Boswell's love stories for us, but none more so than **LANDSLIDE VICTORY**, LOVESWEPT #117. This was a special book for me as I grew up in Washington, D.C. and it evoked lots of pleasant memories. Stacey Lipton is the willful, independent daughter of a conservative Senator, who wants to run for the

(continued)

Presidency; Justin Marks is the Senator's chief aide and chief mainstay in preserving the Lipton family image (no small job with that group of siblings!). When devastatingly controlled Justin is finally provoked beyond endurance by Stacey, the smoldering embers erupt! You'll be delighted by who casts the deciding vote for a **LANDSLIDE VICTORY** for love . . . and just how the "election" takes place . . . in this latest of Barbara's string of real winners!

Evocative, whimsical, and very, very romantic is **HIS FAIR LADY,** LOVESWEPT #118 by Nancy Holder. Claire van Teiler is a craftswoman who travels with a Renaissance Fair and her first introduction to Jack Youngblood almost boggles the gorgeous man's mind! She is a living fantasy in medieval garb chasing her runaway unicorn! (You read that correctly—unicorn!) Jack is a horsebreeder who longs to carry her off on his horse and when he does . . . in the moonlight . . . to a sylvan glade . . . you'll be delighted by the result! Still, there is her young sister Amy and a host of other real world problems for Claire to contend with before she can find her happily-ever-after with Jack. This is another superlatively dreamy and captivatingly different love story from Nancy that, as always, you won't want to miss!

Have a wonderful romantic reading month with LOVESWEPT and with Sandra Brown's historical novel, **ANOTHER DAWN,** on sale now.

Enjoy!

Sincerely,

Carolyn Nichols

Carolyn Nichols
    Editor
LOVESWEPT
Bantam Books, Inc.
666 Fifth Avenue
New York, NY 10103

Dear Reader:

As you know, our goal is to give you a "keeper" with every love story we publish. In our view a "keeper" blends the traditional beloved elements of a romance with truly original ingredients of characterization or plot or setting. Breaking new ground can be risky, but it's well worth it when one succeeds. We hope we succeed almost all the time. Now, well on the road to our third anniversary, we would appreciate a progress report from you. Please take a moment to let us know how you think we're doing.

1. Overall the quality of our stories has *improved* ☐
   declined ☐
   remained the same ☐

2. Would you trust us to increase the number of books we publish each month without sacrificing quality?   *yes* ☐   *no* ☐

3. How many romances do you buy each month? _____

4. Which romance brands do you regularly read?

   _____

   _____

   _____

   _____

   _____

   _____

   I choose my books by author, not brand name ☐

5. Please list your three favorite authors from other lines:

6. Please list your six favorite LOVESWEPT authors:

7. Would you be interested in buying reprinted editions of your favorite LOVESWEPT authors' romances published in the early months of the line?

8. Is there a special message you have for us? (Attach a page, if necessary.)

   With our thanks to you for taking the time and trouble to respond,

Sincerely,

Carolyn Nichols

Carolyn Nichols—for everyone at LOVESWEPT

AN UNTAMED WOMAN . . .
A FEARLESS MAN . . .
A MAGNIFICENT LOVE.
THE MONUMENTAL ADVENTURE
THAT SWEEPS ACROSS A MIGHTY
CENTURY OF AMERICAN HISTORY.

The first time Gavin Ramsay sees Tessa Macleod y Amarista—a violet-eyed beauty swimming naked in a hidden pool—she reacts by attacking him with a knife. Realizing her mistake, she nurses him back to health and into a deep, enduring and courageous love. Together, despite tremendous obstacles, Gavin and Tessa pursue their golden dream—they tame the land, raise a family, and reap great wealth and power. A vast empire is theirs, yet greater still is the magnificent family dynasty they have begun—a dynasty that will flourish on their firm foundation of love.

Passionate, colorful and peopled with unforgettable characters, *The Proud Breed* vividly recreates California's exciting past, from the wild country to the pirated coast, from gambling dens to lavish ballrooms, from the rush for gold to the triumph of statehood. Here an excerpt from Celeste De Blasis' beloved bestselling novel—a world you will not want to leave, and will never forget.

THE PROUD
BREED

He was tired and hungry, and he forgot both when he saw the girl in the pool. He rubbed his eyes; the figure remained, black hair spreading out on the water, slender brown arms cutting the surface with long, easy strokes as she swam. He stared harder. Her body beneath the water gleamed whitely, many shades lighter than the tan of her arms. He could not see her face, but he could imagine it—long slanting dark eyes and the high cheekbones set in the wide face of mixed Indian-Spanish heritage, light and dark which came in countless combinations. She could be nothing else. Daughters of the ruling class did not swim nude and unattended anywhere, anytime.

He smiled to himself. He would be willing to pay just about any price she asked. From what he'd seen so far, she would be worth it. He hadn't had a woman since he'd left Soledad at San Diego. His eyes searched the surrounding area intently. He was sure no one was with her. He began to move quietly down the bank toward her clothes.

Tessa had seen the man when his shadow had fallen briefly across the water before he had stepped into the broken shade. She had thought with sudden terror that it was Luis come to spy upon her, but it was not Luis; the man's build was wrong, wrong for any man on the rancho. A stranger, a man who carried a rifle as though it were an extension of his arm, a man who did not call out reassurance or turn away to allow her to reach her clothes, a man who was coming stealthily down the bank intending harm. She had killed rattlesnakes before, and once a puma which had killed a promising colt. She had no gun now, but the knife would do if she could reach it. Her fear was fast becoming white-hot rage. Her strong strokes carried her to the ledge, her feet found it, and she was out of the pool.

He saw her sudden swiftness, and he increased his own pace. He called to her in Spanish, his laughter making his words nonsensical. Indian would never believe he had seen such a creature in the wilderness of California. He was still thinking about Indian's reaction when he caught up with the girl. She whirled around, and he had only a split second to see she had a lethal-looking knife and eyes the color of wild violets before the blade flashed, aimed to gouge between his ribs and find his heart. He ducked, trying to avoid it, and it plunged deep into his shoulder.

The pain surprised him. It burned down his arm, and when the arm went numb, the pain stayed alive, spreading down his chest into his vitals. The quick warm blood flowing over his skin was a different sensation. He found himself sinking slowly to his knees, and then the girl pushed him backwards and he was lying flat on the ground. He saw her hands moving toward the knife and he tried to roll away, but she was too quick, and he swore violently as she jerked the knife from his shoulder, using both hands. He tried to get his legs under him, knowing she could slit his throat easily as he lay there, but his limbs seemed incapable of responding.

Her voice rang out, sharp and commanding. "Lie still. You are bleeding badly. I won't kill you now."

A rueful grin touched his drawn face. "I don't think you'll have to. I can do this on my own. Perfect English, eyes like flowers, lady, why didn't you just say No?"

"Because I had no way of knowing whether you are a

reasonable man or not. What would you have done in my place?"

"Same thin'." His words were slurring, and his eyes were closed.

"You will let me touch you, let me stop the bleeding?" She took his silence for affirmation and knew he was too weak to resist anyway. She worked quickly, tearing a strip from her petticoat and dipping it into the cool water of the pool, returning to the man to pull the blood-soaked shirt away from the wound and to press the cold dressing against the ugly gash. He came to with a groan when she touched him, but then his jaw clamped shut, and he bore her ministrations in silence. She found the vessel in his neck and pressed down on it with the thumb of her free hand, feeling the hard ridge of his collar bone and the pulsing of his blood, Marías voice telling her, "You can stop the bleeding in this way," María's hands showing her how.

She didn't know how long she stayed like that, crouched over him, blood flowing through the cloth beneath her hand while the other hand used fierce pressure to stop the flow. She became aware of separate and strange things. She had an instant's vision of herself clothed only in the man's blood, nearly impossible to explain to Ramón or any of the *vaqueros* without hastening the man's death. Yet she would give almost anything to have Ramón find her now. There was no way for her to get the man down the hill and home without help. But if the whole episode were to happen again, she would do the same thing. She had had only the advantages of her speed and the knife he hadn't seen. He had had a rifle and far superior strength. She had been taught from childhood that while survival was not always beautiful, it was always desirable. Now the advantage was hers, and it made perfect sense to her that she should be working as fiercely to save his life as she had to take it. Of the man himself she knew nothing except that by his speech he was a Yankee and he had blue eyes. She had only become aware of the blueness after she had stabbed him and he had fallen. They were such a dark blue, they looked black. Strangers passed through so seldom, foreigners even less often; what was he doing here?

Her attention focused again on the wound. The bleeding seemed to have stopped, and she moved her hands away carefully, watching intently. She gave a sigh of satisfaction; there was no new stream of crimson.

His eyes opened slowly. They were very, very blue, but the light was gone from them, and the pupils were enormous. And not even the weathered brown of his skin could hide the pallor beneath. The shadows around his mouth were faint echoes of the color of his eyes. His skin was beaded with sweat, and though the day was warm, his face was cold and clammy to her touch. She could barely find the faint race of his pulse. He moved restlessly and seemed to be making an effort to focus on her. She didn't think he was having much success, and she spoke to him as though he were a small child. "You mustn't move. You must stay very still. Do you hear me?"

The blue gaze sharpened for an instant before his eyes closed again, and he was still save for the small shivers which shook his body involuntarily. She emptied the deerskin pouch he carried, praying she would find more than ammunition there; otherwise, it would take so long. She found it—the flint and steel any good traveler carried. She found something else too, a small package bearing her name and her great-grandfather's seal. She dropped it as though it were the fire she sought, but her mind kept on carrying it as she collected the best tinder and the driest wood she could find and lined the soon crackling heap with stones. The package was her birthday gift, but why had it come with this man? Perhaps he had stolen it—and left it unopened with her name on it? No sense in that. There was only one explanation—Don Esteban had trusted the man to carry the package for him. She closed her eyes and shuddered, imagining what her great-grandfather would think if he could see the outcome.

She had built the fire as close to the man as she dared, and she used his buckskin pouch to protect her hands as she lifted the hot stones and placed them around him, hoping they would give him some warmth. She worked hard, finding additional stones, reheating the original ones as they cooled. She gathered moss from the pool and carried it swiftly to the man, dripping the water on his mouth, watching in relief as his mouth opened and he swallowed thirstily.

His color was better, his pulse stronger; his breathing was deep and he was no longer shivering when she ceased her labors. Her skin was slick with her sweat and his blood, and she couldn't stand either. The icy water of the pool felt heavenly even for the brief time of bathing. When she emerged she put on her clothes before she picked up the package from Don Esteban. Even in this secluded place, she could feel his presence.

Her hands were shaking as she unwrapped it. The collar of emeralds set in gold smoldered with green embers even in the half light of the glade, another world, another time. The beautiful Spanish script spanned past and present. "This was your grandmother's. It should have been your mother's. Now it is yours." No words of love, all words of love. Tears pricked her eyelids, and she looked up to find the blue eyes watching her.

"Please," he said, "whatever else, that must be delivered to the right person. Her name is there." His voice was stronger than it had been.

"It has been delivered. Don Esteban is my great-grandfather," Tessa said.

She could see him fading in and out from the present, and it hit her suddenly. She had wounded him grievously with that first and only thrust, but he was a big man, and by the look of his muscles a strong one.

She bent over him again and asked sharply, "How long since you've eaten?"

He looked up at her. "I like you better with no clothes," he said hazily.

She ignored his comment and the blush that warmed her skin. "How long?"

He screwed up his eyes, thinking for a moment before he answered. "Yesterday, sometime. I was in a hurry."

"You stupid man," Tessa said. "No wonder I had such an easy time of it."

She opened María's package. The woman had provided well for her as always. There were tortillas, strips of beef, and an ample handful of dried fruit.

At first he didn't want anything, but when Tessa threatened to cram it down his throat, he changed his mind. She fed him one small bit at a time, repeatedly cautioning him to chew and swallow carefully. She brought him more water, and she watched his color improve minute by minute.

"There's a flask of brandy in my saddlebags," he said when he had finished eating, and he told her where his horse was.

She stood looking down at him. "I will go, but you must promise not to move. I have your word?"

The smile came again. "You have it. I don't quite feel up to running away yet."

On the opposite slope from where Amordoro grazed, she found the horse, a big chestnut with flaxen mane and tail, and she found the flask and a tin cup. She also found a small bag of salt which she took back with the rest of her booty.

She filled the cup with water first and added a little salt. "This won't taste very good, but you will drink it before I give you anything else."

He made a face but drank it meekly. He drank the brandy with more pleasure.

"Señor, sir . . . I don't even know your name."

"Gavin, Gavin Ramsay."

"It's a strange name, but I like it. I am Tessa Macleod." She could hear Don Esteban saying the Anglo name.

The blue eyes gleamed with life again. "That isn't what was written on the package."

"No, but it is my name," she said firmly, and then her voice softened. "Your wound, there is danger of it poisoning the blood. Sometimes strong spirits help. But I don't have the strength to hold you, and if you move suddenly, the wound may open again."

"I'll hold still," he said, and she knew he would. Even lying there helpless, Gavin Ramsay radiated power. The name kept repeating itself in her mind, an important name not to be forgotten.

She did not want to remove the blood pad that covered the wound for fear of starting the bleeding again, so she poured the liquor liberally onto the covering and around the edges. His breath hissed out of his tightly clenched mouth, sweat sprang out on his skin, and his hands were doubled into fists, but he did not move.

Gavin felt the world would burst into flame, agony streaked through his body, and then he felt gentle hands stroking his face, a soft voice crooning to him. The pain eased back to the throbbing in his shoulder, and his tight muscles began to relax. He could still feel her hands and hear her voice when he drifted off.

Tessa watched him as he slept. She had never seen such a man. Don Esteban, Luis, her father, they were all tall, around six feet, as were many Californio men, but this man was taller and much broader in the shoulders than the others, though he had the lean hips and long legs of a horseman. His hair was as black as her own, and the lashes that shielded the blue eyes were long and thick enough to be the envy of any woman. But there was nothing feminine about his face. Even in sleep, his mouth had the hard, firm line that reminded her of Don Esteban. His cheekbones were high and prominent, emphasizing the hollows beneath; his nose was strong and straight; his chin and jawline left no doubt about where the bones were. And his body showed hard usage. A faint line of white ran across his right cheekbone, a scar that would not darken like the rest of his skin. And hers would not be the first scar on his chest. She wondered what his life had been to leave him so marked.

He stirred restlessly and his eyes opened, staring blankly

at her until he remembered. "We can't stay here forever," he said. "I think I can ride now."

She held him down by his good shoulder when she saw he intended to get up. "No. We will wait here. My men know where I am. They will come for me. It will take time because I have ordered them to leave me alone. But Ramón will disobey. He always does when he worries." Her voice allowed no argument, but her next words were more tentative. "I have thought about it. When they come I will tell them I found you so. You had a fight with another man. He was gone when I found you. You must pretend this is true. They are protective of me, you understand? If they knew the truth, they might undo all the work I have done to keep you in this world, and I don't think you are ready to go to the next. I think perhaps you would go to the wrong place."

Gavin agreed, trying not to laugh. "But do you think they will believe you?" he asked. "I wouldn't."

"You would if you were one of my men and I said such was true," Tessa state flatly, and Gavin smiled again. He had had more than enough time to study the girl, helpless as he'd been in her hands, and her spirit and her arrogant self-possession would have done a middle-aged matriarch proud. She was obviously accustomed to giving orders and to being obeyed, but her body betrayed her youth. She was tall for a woman, but she still had a coltish delicacy which showed in the quick way she moved and in the slenderness of her limbs and neck. Her breasts were small, upthrusting promises of things yet to be, and her hips were scarcely wider than a boy's. Oh, yes, he'd seen her quite clearly and he knew the wiry strength that lay beneath her fragility. There was something undeniably sensual about this child woman, something as basically sexual as the smell, feel, and movement of all earth things. He realized he'd been staring because he could see the blood rising to darken her golden skin. Those eyes, he had never seen eyes that color before. "How old are you?" he asked abruptly.

"Today I am sixteen years old," she said proudly, and

her anger flashed when she saw him grin. "It is not so young! Of course, you are probably a very old man, so it seems young to you."

"I am. I'm twenty-six, or thereabouts, and I feel as if I'm sixty today."

Tessa made him drink some water and allowed him more brandy, and he fell asleep again. The afternoon was growing later, but she never doubted Ramón would come. She heard him calling her before he appeared at the top of the rise, and she went to meet him. She quieted his apologies for coming to find her by putting her arms around him and kissing his leathery cheek. "I've never been so glad to see anyone in my life! I'm all right, but there is a man who is badly hurt. I found him here, and I need help to get him home."

They carried him down the hill as carefully as they could, watching their footing against a sliding fall, Tessa doggedly holding up her corner of the blanket. There wasn't a sound from Gavin, and Tessa thought he had fainted until his eyes opened under the intensity of her gaze. She realized suddenly how much it hurt his pride to be so helpless, a hurt worse than the physical, which was something he could bear. This man was not used to being at the mercy of others. She smiled at him and turned her attention back to the ground.

Jesus! he thought, it's a good thing I didn't see that smile before, I might have taken her after all. His idea that she was a child was forgotten. The smile had transformed her face, making it luminous, ageless, and more beautiful than any face he had ever seen. He knew she had not lied about the fever; he could feel it taking him beyond reason on endless waves of warmth. He was only sorry the pain followed him. He concentrated on Tessa until he saw nothing but her smile, felt nothing except the slender body cradling him against the jolts, her hands touching, holding him, heard nothing save the comfort of her voice.

LOVESWEPT

Love Stories you'll never forget by authors you'll always remember

☐	21603	**Heaven's Price** #1 Sandra Brown	$1.95
☐	21604	**Surrender** #2 Helen Mittermeyer	$1.95
☐	21600	**The Joining Stone** #3 Noelle Berry McCue	$1.95
☐	21601	**Silver Miracles** #4 Fayrene Preston	$1.95
☐	21605	**Matching Wits** #5 Carla Neggers	$1.95
☐	21606	**A Love for All Time** #6 Dorothy Garlock	$1.95
☐	21609	**Hard Drivin' Man** #10 Nancy Carlson	$1.95
☐	21611	**Hunter's Payne** #12 Joan J. Domning	$1.95
☐	21618	**Tiger Lady** #13 Joan Domning	$1.95
☐	21614	**Brief Delight** #15 Helen Mittermeyer	$1.95
☐	21639	**The Planting Season** #33 Dorothy Garlock	$1.95
☐	21627	**The Trustworthy Redhead** #35 Iris Johansen	$1.95

Prices and availability subject to change without notice.

Buy them at your local bookstore or use this handy coupon for ordering:

Bantam Books, Inc., Dept. SW, 414 East Golf Road, Des Plaines, Ill. 60016

Please send me the books I have checked above. I am enclosing $_____ (please add $1.25 to cover postage and handling). Send check or money order —no cash or C.O.D.'s please.

Mr/Mrs/Miss_____

Address_____

City_____State/Zip_____

SW—10/85

Please allow four to six weeks for delivery. This offer expires 4/86.

SPECIAL
MONEY SAVING
OFFER

Now you can have an up-to-date listing of Bantam's hundreds of titles plus take advantage of our unique and exciting bonus book offer. A special offer which gives you the opportunity to purchase a Bantam book for only 50¢. Here's how!

By ordering any five books at the regular price per order, you can also choose any other single book listed (up to a $4.95 value) for just 50¢. Some restrictions do apply, but for further details why not send for Bantam's listing of titles today!

Just send us your name and address plus 50¢ to defray the postage and handling costs.

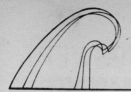

LOVESWEPT

*Love Stories you'll never forget
by authors you'll always remember*

Prices and availability subject to change without notice.

Buy them at your local bookstore or use this handy coupon for ordering:

LOVESWEPT

Love Stories you'll never forget by authors you'll always remember

☐	21682	**The Count from Wisconsin #75** Billie Green	$2.25
☐	21683	**Tailor-Made #76** Elizabeth Barrett	$2.25
☐	21684	**Finders Keepers #77** Nancy Holder	$2.25
☐	21688	**Sensuous Perception #78** Barbara Boswell	$2.25
☐	21686	**Thursday's Child #79** Sandra Brown	$2.25
☐	21691	**The Finishing Touch #80** Joan Elliott Pickart	$2.25
☐	21685	**The Light Side #81** Joan Bramsch	$2.25
☐	21689	**White Satin #82** Iris Johansen	$2.25
☐	21690	**Illegal Possession #83** Kay Hooper	$2.25
☐	21693	**A Stranger Called Adam #84** B. J. James	$2.25
☐	21700	**All the Tomorrows #85** Joan Elliott Pickart	$2.25
☐	21692	**Blue Velvet #86** Iris Johansen	$2.25
☐	21661	**Dreams of Joe #87** Billie Green	$2.25
☐	21702	**At Night Fall #88** Joan Bramsch	$2.25
☐	21694	**Captain Wonder #89** Anne Kolaczyk	$2.25
☐	21703	**Look for the Sea Gulls #90** Joan Elliott Pickart	$2.25
☐	21704	**Calhoun and Kid #91** Sara Orwig	$2.25
☐	21705	**Azure Days, Quicksilver Nights #92** Carole Douglas	$2.25
☐	21697	**Practice Makes Perfect #93** Kathleen Downes	$2.25
☐	21706	**Waiting for Prince Charming #94** Joan Elliott Pickart	$2.25
☐	21707	**Darling Obstacles #95** Barbara Boswell	$2.25
☐	21695	**Enchantment #86** Kimberli Wagner	$2.25
☐	21698	**What's A Nice Girl . . . ? #97** Adrienne Staff & Sally Goldenbaum	$2.25
☐	21701	**Mississippi Blues #98** Fayrene Preston	$2.25

Prices and availability subject to change without notice.

Buy them at your local bookstore or use this handy coupon for ordering:

Bantam Books, Inc., Dept. SW4, 414 East Golf Road, Des Plaines, Ill. 60016

Please send me the books I have checked above. I am enclosing $_____ (please add $1.25 to cover postage and handling). Send check or money order—no cash or C.O.D.'s please.

Mr/Ms_____

Address _____

City/State_____ Zip_____

SW4—10/85

Please allow four to six weeks for delivery. This offer expires 4/86.